GW00383110

FROST FAIR

Frost Fair

Erastes

Cheyenne Publishing
Camas, Washington
www.cheyennepublishing.com

FROST FAIR. Copyright © 2008, 2009 by Erastes
All rights reserved. No part of this publication may be
reproduced, restored in a retrieval system, or transmitted in any
form or by any means, electronic, mechanical, photocopying,
recording or otherwise, without the prior written permission of
the publisher.

ISBN: 978-0-9797773-2-5

Cover art by Alex Beecroft

Published by Cheyenne Publishing
Camas, Washington
Mailing Address:
    P. O. Box 872412 Vancouver, WA 98687-2412
Website: www.cheyennepublishing.com

Other books by Erastes from Cheyenne Publishing:

Speak Its Name: A Trilogy (segment, *Hard and Fast*)

Books by other authors from Cheyenne Publishing:

The Filly by Mark R. Probst

The Royal Navy Series by Lee Rowan:
Ransom
Winds of Change
Eye of the Storm

Walking Wounded by Lee Rowan

Hidden Conflict: Tales from Lost Voices in Battle

For Tracey, who understood Gideon long before I did.

CHAPTER ONE

"And I assure *you*, Mr. Malter, that as soon as I have the money, you will have it, before I've had a chance to buy even so much as a pastry." Gideon Frost "assisted" the paper merchant's agent out of the tiny printer's shop and closed the door on him, locked it and pulled down the blind. Then the smile he'd been holding throughout the interview with the increasingly irate clerk slid from his face as slowly and surely as snow slipping from a roof. The man could still be heard outside, complaining of the debt-ridden printer and his shoddy work to anyone who might be listening. Gideon stayed quiet, waiting until he eventually heard the man's footsteps and complaining voice fading away.

He was grateful that Simeon & Sons had sent such a small and easily manhandled debt-collector, but he knew that he'd been lucky in that. He would not remain so for long.

As he walked back through the shop into the claustrophobic working space-cum-bedroom, Gideon rubbed his chilled hands together and tried to regain the good humour he'd had before Malter's visit. Debts. Too many debts and these days, too many debt-collectors. He had no doubt that this one was nothing more than a shot across the bows. The fussy little Malter would bear no relation to the man that, Gideon was sure, would be along later today, or at the latest tomorrow. The next one would be bigger, a lot bigger, and probably armed. Things had become desperate. Money had to be found, and fast.

He hated closing the shop, but it had to be done. The likelihood of selling an engraving or a lithograph this late in the day was utterly remote. It was late January, and few people were interested in buying such luxuries after the excesses of Christmas; and the daylight, already muted by the dark grey sky, was fading fast, making the few people that were around drift away, no doubt thinking of hearth and home.

Locking up, Gideon made his way through the narrow shop-lined streets, wincing as the bitter ice-chilled wind cut through the layers of clothing right through to his bones. He couldn't remember when it had been as cold as this; icicles hung from every roof and the frost hung around in the streets long after daylight broke. The sun was almost constantly hidden by black, menacing clouds, keeping the temperatures down. A fog was building too, rising from the frozen ground, creeping along the quiet alleys. *It will be thick by tonight,* Gideon thought.

Frost's shop was near the Strand end of Fleet Street—a decent location for passing trade and for visitors to the prisons—but it was a freezing walk from there to St Paul's, and before he'd even reached Ludgate Hill, he was chilled to the bone and not in any mood for the business he had come about.

Damn it, he thought, *another few pennies are not going to beggar me.* With a wry smile at his own delusions he stepped inside The Bell, nodding to his father's acquaintances—printers and journalists, to a man—and slid down into a shadowed booth with his tankard.

Acquaintances, he thought to himself. *Not friends.* His fingers tightened around his mug at the memory of how no one had raised a finger to help his father when he'd got ill, despite Gideon being sent around the area with pleas for aid. *Anything would have done,* he thought. *We didn't want food, or paper. Just someone to run the press until his arm was healed.*

Gideon had tried, but he'd been too young to run the business well enough for the both of them. He didn't have the breadth of acquaintance that his father did, nor the easy charm, being less garrulous and a lot shyer than his open-handed father. Mr. Frost senior's talent was for engraving, and between the bread-and-butter printing work (there were always pamphlets being printed by some wit, wag or Whig), and Gideon's pictures of London scenes and the occasional commission of a portrait, the little shop had just managed to keep its head above water. That was until Gideon's father had caught his arm in the press. The wound had festered and, in the end, it had killed him.

Gideon had constantly to remind himself that it was the press and the infected arm that had killed him, not his father's printing peers, but he found it hard not to feel bitter. His father had often loaned a fellow printer some ink, some paper, some skill in repairing the mechanism. He hadn't been a saint, far from it, but he had helped others.

At the pathetic, sparse burial, Gideon hadn't spoken to anyone. He had been too angry. And when all the debts were paid, and he realised he'd nothing left except the press, he swore to himself that he'd never ask a man for help—not if he died in consequence.

Outside the grimy windows of the inn he could see that the light had finally gone, so he pulled on his gloves and went back out into the street. As anticipated, the fog was thicker now; already it was almost impossible to see the other side of the street. As he strode up Ludgate Hill, St Paul's loomed, ghostly and white, over the area. The uphill walk and the ale had warmed him a little and he was more prepared for his work as he reached the Churchyard. There were already a couple of figures in the shadows moving away from the street, and Gideon thought he might be lucky. St Paul's Churchyard, with its proximity to the mighty cathedral, seemed, at first glance, an unlikely place for male prostitution, but it was well-established. There were other places, Gideon knew, but the theatres cost money, and Cock Lane and Lad Lane were too damned far in this cold. Besides, more gentlemen came to this area. Perhaps not aristocracy—at least Gideon had never knowingly encountered any—but there were men with money to spend for a talented hand or mouth.

The proximity of the great church seemed to thin the fog, so he slipped into the deeper shadows on the cathedral side and walked as quietly as he could along the path around the edge. His nerves always set in when he was this close to selling himself. Fear of meeting someone violent, fear of the constables, fear of meeting someone he knew. Here and there under the trees he could make out shapes, moving furtively and no doubt engaging in the minimum of small talk before commencing their activities.

Behind the Chapter House, dark and secluded, there was a paved, small courtyard and Gideon made for that. He knew damned well that men sold themselves even during the day here, and indeed in St Paul's Walk, and even within the walls of the Cathedral itself, but he had not sunk that far—yet. Sometimes he wondered if one day it might come to that, because he never seemed to make enough money honestly.

In the courtyard, the fog parted to reveal a tall man, cloaked, wearing a high buckled hat. Whether he was offering trade or waiting for it, Gideon didn't yet know, but he stepped quietly in, moving softly towards the dark figure, his heart pounding in his chest. It wasn't unheard of for constables to lay in wait for the "unnaturals" that frequented the Churchyard, but Gideon had come too far to stop now, and the thought of another debt collector's visit drove him on. He fancied he knew this part of London as well as any Bow Street Runner, and he was fitter and leaner than most of them; he'd give them a run for their money before he'd allow himself to be caught.

The man was smoking a pipe, and the glow lit his face with an unearthly hue, highlighting a broad forehead, decorated with fashionable curls, and a slim, rapacious nose. Not handsome, but not bracket-faced, either. Gideon steeled himself.

"Good evening, sir," he said, then, realising how damned loud his voice sounded, he pitched it lower, and added a more common slant to his tone. "Lonely?"

"I have been waiting for company," the man said, "and the wind is so chill I've damned near lost the use of what I'd use."

"I think that you will need to be warmed then, sir," Gideon said, stepping closer. The scent of the pipe was warm and pleasant, redolent of roaring fires and spicy ale. They were inches apart; the man did not back away and Gideon knew the dance from here. His hand touched the man's jacket, then dropped lower to find with annoyance and surprise that the man hadn't even readied himself, and was still buttoned up. "I thought you'd be ready for me, sir," he said to cover his annoyance.

"Oh I am," said the stranger. "You'll see." The pipe flared again and Gideon felt a shiver of fear.

Perhaps the man *was* a constable, perhaps this was one visit too many. But in the light of the dying embers of the pipe, Gideon could see the man had a small smile, as if he'd just realised what Gideon meant.

"Oh it's my first time here," the man continued. Gideon rather doubted that, but a lot of the sodomites gave that excuse, if they talked at all. "And in any case, I fear your hands might be colder than my piece," he said, and Gideon felt a gloved hand catch hold of one of his own. "Dash it, even through my gloves I can tell. Veritable blocks of ice. What is your name?"

Confused, Gideon backed away, shaking his hand loose. This was not how things were supposed to go. Other visits here had been almost wordless; an exchange, a dicker for price, a swift fumble, palm tight around prick to conclusion and a hurried parting. That was the tradition, the steps of the dance. Some men did more—out there in the dark he could hear unmistakable grunting that told a tale of a hurried, cold coupling—but Gideon never let anyone swive him for money.

"No names here, sir. If I don't suit, I'll..."

"No." The man knocked out his pipe against the wall. "Damn me. I had thought this would be more of an adventure, and all I am is freezing. Come. Let me make you a proposition. We can continue here, you can stroke my *arbor vitae* for me with those cold hands for a shilling—or you can come have a drink with me and rouse me thoroughly. For a guinea. Whaddyousay? Blamed if I'm standing around in the cold—even for a handling—when there's comfort to be had."

The air seemed colder; the fog left droplets of moisture on their clothes, which froze as soon as they formed and the snow had started at last. Gideon was sorely tempted at the offer. A guinea. He'd come up here to make a few shillings but a guinea could buy off Simeon and some left for those inks he'd been promising himself... But to go off with some stranger, no matter how rich he seemed, was madness.

"Go where, sir?"

"Good man," the stranger said.

"Wait, I did not agree—"

"Who's there?"

Both men turned as one as the new voice cut through the snow and the fog. A lantern, held aloft by what Gideon was quite certain was an unseen constable, was moving through the dark. "The Yard's being searched," he hissed to his companion. "We need to leave. *Now.*"

Angry voices echoed off the cathedral walls. "'Ere! What are you two about? Grab 'im—*and* 'im!" It seemed the Runners had found a couple who had wasted less time in conversation than Gideon and his erstwhile customer. All thoughts of debts and guineas temporarily vanished; he grabbed his companion's arm and together they sped out of the gate as fast as was possible, keeping in the darkest shadows until they were into the main street where they melted into the fog and walked slowly away towards the river. Gideon's heart was pounding; it was the closest he'd come to that kind of danger.

"I'll leave you here," he said, too scared by the experience to keep his voice subservient. "Good hunting, sir."

"No, wait—" The gentleman caught hold of his arm, and Gideon turned. The lantern nearest to them threw light and detail upon a friendly and a younger face than Gideon was expecting. "My carriage is just below, in Carter Lane."

Gideon was impressed in spite of himself, but wondered why such a man as this needed to frequent such a whore-pit as St Paul's. The man continued, "I meant it, about the guinea. A meal, some drink..."

"Another time, sir, I'm afraid."

"Just to thank you, then? You saved us both back there while I was blind in the dark. Your knowledge of the Churchyard...Oh...put my foot in it."

Gideon flinched. He wasn't used to people discussing his whoring to his face.

"Damn," the man continued. He leant forward, took Gideon's hand, and shook it. "I'm always saying the wrong thing. But the offer's there if you want."

"It's kind of you, but I think we have risked enough tonight."

"Another time then, as you say."

Without an answer—for who wants to make friends with a customer?—Gideon turned on his heel, stuck his hands back into his gloves and strode towards home, cursing himself. *And what was your stiff-necked reason for turning away a guinea? He didn't look dangerous, or diseased.* He berated himself all the way back down the hill, which took his mind off the cold, at least. He knew why he hadn't taken the seemingly pleasant young man up on his offer. It was because the man would expect...everything. Everything for a guinea. And everything was something Gideon didn't sell.

Now, he thought bitterly, *you'll have to walk to Lad Lane and be lucky with a couple of shillings unless you want to lose everything.* Without thought he pushed open the door to The Bell once more, wanting a bracer before the walk, pulled out his change, noted the unaccustomed weight and stared, unbelieving, at his palm. There in the centre of his last pennies was a bright, brassy and quite beautiful guinea.

CHAPTER TWO

Back in his shop, Gideon put a little coal on the fire, then carefully put the guinea in a little box on the mantelpiece. His thoughts were ragged, disorganised. He hadn't earned it. He hadn't done anything. But then...treacherous thoughts passed through his mind. He didn't know the man, and the likelihood of seeing him again was remote. He was nearly certain that he would have handed it back if he'd known it was there. Or he would have gone with the man and attempted to negotiate the extent and the price of his services. But, he reasoned, he had got them both out of there before the Runners widened their search. A grateful guinea was probably nothing to a man with that quality of clothes. Gideon remembered the feel of the thick woollen coat under his fingers, and the mention of a carriage left idling in Carter's.

Gratitude, then. An expression of gratitude.

After all, that's where "gratuity" came from, wasn't it? He wasn't certain of his facts on the linguistics, but it seemed to make sense.

That evening, for the first in many, he filled the grate, then banked the fire so it would smoulder slowly through the night.

When Gideon woke the next morning, the fire had made a wonderful difference in the little room. He opened his eyes and his face was warm, the first time since sometime in October. He found that he'd actually thrown off his bed jacket in the night and he could feel Muffin, the cat that he pretended he didn't live with, curled up at the end of the bed, a warm heavy weight on his toes. He lay there in the cocooning dark for a moment or two before taking a tinder box from the floor beside him and striking a match for his lamp.

He was busy planning his day, washing and shaving when he heard a familiar repeated knock at the front door. Not bothering to wipe the foam from his face, he opened the door. Snow came billowing out of the fog, and even the fog itself seemed to creep into the shop in menacing floor-level tendrils. It took a moment to force the door closed again, while the bell above the door clanged wildly. With a shudder for the chill that had invaded the warmth of the shop, he turned to the small figure peeling its coat off and bending to stroke Muffin, who usually ignored all humans (including Gideon) but for some reason tolerated the worship of a young guttersnipe.

"Mornin', guvnor."

Half-suspecting that the boy was actually talking to the cat, Gideon chose to claim the greeting for himself.

"Good morning, Mord. You are early."

"Not finished your shave, yet?"

"As you can see."

"Yeah. Sorry, guv. Our Mum sent me down to the river with our Easy and our Urry to see if it was freezing."

"It's cold enough for it." He continued his shave. "Any sign of it?"

"I think this year it just might, you know? The jetties and banks is all frozen already, and some of the boats is stuck fast. An' they've had to break the ice between the arches on the bridge twice, Old Isaac told us. There's big lumps of ice floating in the water, too big and too dang'rous for the boatmen to fish out and when they hit the bridges? The sound is fair like old Boney's cannons."

Gideon wiped his face. "Pray that you may never hear the real thing. Your mother is putting money on it freezing." It wasn't a question. She did it every year.

"Of course!" The boy grinned, now holding Muffin who had a patient expression on its grizzled face. *If I tried that,* thought Gideon, *the animal would take my nose off.* "Coo—wouldn't it be good though? I've seen pictures but Ma would be the first one down there with her cart, waiting for the crowds."

"Personally," Gideon said dryly, pulling wrapped engraving plates from a drawer, "after this month, I wouldn't say no to some warmer weather. I don't know if I would trust the ice, especially with a heavy cart. You would last about a minute in that cold if you fell in."

"Worth the risk, Ma says. She told us about the last time it froze. Only for a day, she said, but everyone went rushing over there. People fell in too, didn't put people off. It's warm in here though. 'Ad some luck yesterday, did ya?'"

Turning away and sitting down at the bench, Gideon nodded. "Yes. A bit of luck. Put the kettle on, will you? The heat won't last forever and we might as well get some food in us before the fire dies. And put that flea-carrier out, she'll only start scratching the door when I get the inks out, and the varnish is hardly dry from last time." He hoped the boy was offended enough at the insult to his favourite—for Gideon was quite sure the boy was fonder of the cat than he was of his employer—not to question him further on what he'd sold and to whom. "Put her out the back window, though, I don't want to open the front door again until I have to."

Mord did as he was told, then set about getting breakfast for them both.

With a shrug of his shoulders to ease a stiffness, Gideon sat down and started to work on the commission due at the end of the week. It was an engraving of a client's house, newly refurbished and faced with glaring white stone.

Mordecai chattered on as he fried bacon. "You're out of tea," he said, putting a plate in front of Gideon. "Want me to get some when I'm out?"

Gideon covered the engraving over and put it to one side.

"No." No point in pretending they were in a post-Christmas glut. That pretty little guinea had a lot of work to do. "We'll just have to go back to the coffee."

Mordecai wandered off, muttering about how some coffee was no better than floor sweepings, but he didn't press the point. "You made a list?" he called out from the back room. Gideon could hear him putting the bed away and turning the handles of the press for oiling.

"I have," Gideon said, "but if you can manage the shop this morning, I want to go out myself. It's not like we are going to be that busy."

Mordecai came back in, wiping his hands. "I was going to do them leaflets for Doctor Cushing, s'morning."

"They can wait, if he comes in for them, then blame me."

"Fair enough. He don't pay on time anyway, cheap old sod—"

"Mordecai..."

"Well, he is."

"He most certainly is not, although he may be a little parsimonious. Careful. And after all, so am I. Careful, that is," he added hurriedly, glad the boy couldn't see him blush.

"Yeah, well, you ain't got two grigs—sorry, guv—*farthings* to rub together, mostly. He's just a fat cull."

"But not a sod. His wife will attest to that, I'm sure."

Gideon pulled his coat on, and Mordecai turned away grumbling, but with a smile on his face. "I will be back before noon, Mord," he said, "and don't let that cat in."

"Goin' to Simeons'?"

"First thing." Mordecai gave a small look of relief and Gideon left without saying more. He hated that Mord knew about his debts, but it was unavoidable. And he knew the boy worried. Gideon worried too, especially as to what might happen one day if an overanxious debtor came calling when it was just the boy there on his own. He doubted he'd even be able to deal with someone like Malter. It was the main reason he let the boy do the bulk of the shopping for the shop; he somehow felt that, even carrying cash, Mord was safer on the streets than facing down a debt-collector in a confined space.

As with many manufactories, Simeon's warehouse was down on the river; a large building with eaves that overhung the water like a drunken giant. The smell down by the river was usually rancid, speaking to nose and sinus of the effluent poured into the Thames by a hundred, a thousand workshops. Today, Gideon noted, it was less offensive; perhaps it was the fog and the snow keeping it down. He negotiated the ash-strewn cobbled street with care, slipping and sliding until he almost fell through the doorway.

The adventure of the journey had taken his mind from the factory, but when he pulled off his hat and shook the snowflakes free from his ears, he looked into the dim cavernous space and remembered exactly why he hated coming here. There were men hauling trucks around, carrying bolts of paper, but it was the other workers that set Gideon's teeth on edge. Blank-eyed children, some younger than Mord's little brothers, looked back at him, holding his gaze for a second and looking away again, with a frightening lack of curiosity. He felt no guilt for employing Mordecai, for without a job in the relatively clean and safe environment of the printer's shop, he would likely be here, or any one of the manufactories along the diseased river.

Malter came out of a door off the main warehouse. He was smiling, but it was more a case of showing his teeth than any show of pleasure. "Ah, Mr. Frost," he said, and the waves of self-satisfaction that came off him were plain to Gideon's eyes, and did nothing to warm him to the little man's personality. "I am pleased you saw sense."

"How could I not," Gideon said with as much sincerity as the other, "when you were so persuasive?" Better he think that, than know of Gideon's fears of what might come after. Malter opened the door and gestured Gideon through it into a darkly panelled office, bleak as charity and nothing more to catch the eye than an oil lamp on the desk, almost completely obscured by piles of ledgers.

Malter sat down; he didn't need to ask Gideon to sit as there wasn't another chair in the room. As the little man pulled one of the ledgers onto the desk in front of him, Gideon watched, wondering if it was his surroundings that seemed to have desiccated the clerk. Whether it was the constant camouflage of parchment and paper that had dried him out. He wondered briefly if he was married, if someone loved him, if anyone could with his stained fingers, dirty nails and unnaturally yellow, wispy hair that lay plastered on his scalp.

He finished writing in a meticulous hand and looked up. "You'll be paying the amount in full?"

"No, actually I won't," Gideon said without a change in his expression.

"You won't? Is that wise, Mr. Frost?"

Gideon put the guinea down on the desk. "I'm paying for half of the quires I owe you for. Then I'll expect eight more delivered, at which point I'll pay for the lot."

Malter was gaping in shock. "You want more credit?"

"It's not all credit. I am paying for some of it."

"Less than half of what you owe, and then want more!"

"I may be slow to pay, Mr. Malter, but I do always pay, I am sure that you have many a customer about which that is not true. I have a commission on hand which will clear the debt in full upon delivery."

There was a fruity laugh from behind him and it took all of Gideon's self-control not to turn and react. Instead, he gave the smallest of yawns, as if he were warm and comfortable and turned his head slowly, unsurprised to see Simeon himself in the doorframe.

"You are a bloody cheeky cub, a veritable Corinthian," Simeon laughed. "I have always said as much. You may not take after your father in a lot of ways but you have a brass neck. Fair enough. I'll deal round with you, lad."

Gideon bit his tongue. Personally, he did not consider threatening his livelihood with disaster was round dealing, but this was not the time to discuss it.

"You agree to my terms?"

"Let us say that you happened to strike on my own terms. When is your commission to be paid?"

"The original is to be delivered to my client on the fourth of February."

"And on the fifth of February?"

"I shall pay my debt to you in full."

"Good lad. And on the sixth day of February you shall have full credit with us once more."

Gideon opened his mouth to speak, but considered that he'd gone as far as he dared. Malter had gone red in the face but he opened a drawer, took out a box and changed Gideon's guinea into smaller denominations then handed a palm full of coins over without another word.

As the owner of the mill held the door open, Gideon slid through it. Then, when Simeon offered him a spit-soaked hand to shake, he dutifully spat likewise; solemnly, and in the centre of his palm, and shook Simeon's large, meaty hand. He refrained from the impulse to wipe his own until he was out of sight of the factory and swallowed up by the fog. Then he did it thoroughly, scrubbing his hands with snow before sticking them back into his gloves and feeling unclean even then.

The fog was so bad on his way home that he

actually got lost and had to step into a shop and find out the name of the road. After that, he kept to the pavement where it was possible, counting off streets in his head, and was relieved when he started to recognise the buildings around him, enabling him to do some of the shopping on his list.

As he pushed open the door of the shop, Mord came rushing to help him with his packages. "Coo, you had me worried. It sounded noon a good while back. You didn't have no trouble—"

Shoving almost all the parcels on the boy to shut him up, Gideon stamped the snow from his feet on the worn mat. "No reason why I should, Mord."

"If you say so, guv'nor."

"I do. Now brush off. Here's the rest of the list. Did Cushing call?"

Mord took the list and held his hand out for the Gideon's purse, which he tied to a leather string around his waist and tucked away inside his breeches. "He did and he weren't too pleased with being given the brush, neither. Said he'd come back for a nexplan-a-tion." Gideon had to turn away at Mord's impression of the pompous doctor, so the boy didn't see his smile. "We didn't sell nothing, neither, so you was lucky yesterday. What you sell anyway?"

"I will speak to him." Gideon gave the basket to the boy and ushered him out before any more questions got asked. He turned up the lamps against the unnatural dark the fog was causing and sat down with the commission that would—he

trusted—get him out of his current financial hole
for at least a month or so.

He sat and stared at the plate, and carefully
wiped off some imaginary dust with a soft cloth.
The house was very beautiful. With eager hands,
he pulled out the sketches that he'd made of the
house as a basis for the engraving. The sketches
were, necessarily, more vibrant than the finished
portrayal would be, an impression of movement in
the handsome imported trees in the frontage and,
most importantly, in one of them a rough and
hurried sketch of the owner himself. Gideon knew
that a casual observer would not think that the
pencilled lines did the man justice, but as he
gazed at the rough drawing he'd done of the man
as he stood outside his house, it seemed to Gideon
himself as if the man was in the room. Gideon
could almost see his light blue eyes, and that dark
hair, with touches of grey already showing at the
temples. Could see the crinkles at his eyes—he
always seemed to be smiling, but then, Gideon
reasoned, with his life—money and nothing but
comfortable living—he had reason to spend his life
smiling. He'd only seen the man twice—once when
he came to the shop and once when he'd gone to
sketch—but Gideon was as lost in admiration and
a hopeless longing as ever he had been in for any
of his school friends. And, like his school friends,
Mr. Joshua Redfern had no idea that anyone had
an unnatural affection for him. Why should he?

The bell to the shop sounded and Gideon
swiftly put a cloth over the plate and the sketches,
mentally steeling himself for excuses to give the

good doctor as to why his pamphlets were not ready. Wiping his hands, he ducked through the door to the shop and stood transfixed and speechless, for it was as if a wish had been granted. For there, seeming to fill the space provided, was the object of Gideon's hopeless affection, Mr. Redfern himself.

CHAPTER THREE

ellsfire, but it was cold. The little shop had tiny windows to the street, but they glowed with a warm, welcoming glow. Outside, Redfern stamped his feet and cursed the weather, unsuitable boots, thin stockings and the gods in general. Most particularly he cursed Matthew, his younger, love-sick brother who had insisted on dragging him from Brooks' (where he'd been up ten guineas) to climb into an uncomfortable, draughty and no doubt flea-ridden public conveyance to Twinings, where he'd heard the divine Miss Devereaux was going to be. Despite Redfern's assurance that no lady would be addled enough to visit a teashop in this weather, no matter how fashionable a pursuit, there was no dissuading Matthew. Then when they arrived, the damned shop was closed.

Matthew had given one of his most pup-like grins in response to Redfern's invective and had suggested a return to Brooks'.

"Not today," Redfern had said. "And you'd better to go home, but I doubt that you will. Now you have dragged me from its doors with my pockets the richer for it, I think I should give Thouless time to plan his revenge."

"He did not look pleased at the defeat."

"And you looked entirely *too* pleased, little brother."

Matthew turned away at that and studied his walking cane with some care. "Not at all, although I admit that I don't like him. Don't like some of the stories."

"What have you heard? Irish gossip?" Redfern said acerbically. "Tattles from scullery maids and governesses. Things beyond The Pale are done differently than in London, Matty. What has he done other than charm and spend money, since he blew in from Kilkenny?"

Matthew had said no more about it, but Redfern was nettled. He liked people to like his friends and Finbarr Thouless was the talk of the *ton*. He'd been pleased when the big, attractive Irishman had singled him out and sought his acquaintance. Redfern had wondered at it, for, other than an independent fortune, he himself had no power or influence. No title and no important relations. Nothing like the sort of person that Thouless seemed to normally gravitate to.

For a very little while he had hoped that Thouless had sought him out for more intimate reasons, because the Irishman *was* damnably handsome with his darkly curling hair and his blue eyes—"put in by a sooty finger" as the saying went—but Redfern was disappointed (as was so often the case) when his new friend appeared to share none of his own interest in the male sex.

He watched the hackney swing away until in no time at all it was swallowed by the fog. He'd not encouraged Matthew to accompany him; the boy was already suspicious of his older brother's bachelorhood, and it would be difficult to explain a visit to the engraver when the tradesman would come to the house whenever summoned. Redfern was also a little afraid that he was so attuned to Frost's blond masculine beauty that anyone looking at himself, looking at the engraver, would be unable to mistake his longing.

For longing it was, from the first time he'd seen the young man a few weeks before. He'd accompanied Finbarr Thouless through these very streets, as the Irishman hunted for a shop he'd heard of that could provide portraits and sketches for "discerning gentlemen" but they got turned around, somehow, in the maze of bookshops and printworks. It didn't help that Thouless and he were rather the worse for drink.

It was Thouless who saw Frost first. Redfern had been browsing through some old atlases, wondering if he should buy them for their historical interest—the world changed shape daily, it seemed—when he became aware of Thouless' sudden stillness and turned to look at his friend. The Irishman had been transfixed by something he'd seen. Redfern had not seen that expression in a man's face before; his eyes had narrowed and his whole body was still, almost leaning towards the object of his gaze. It reminded Redfern of a Pointer bitch he'd owned as a boy. He was just about to laughingly point this out when Thouless seemed to become aware of his behaviour and continued his conversation.

"What was it you were looking at?" Redfern had asked, looking in vain amongst the shopping throng.

"Something rather beautiful," the man answered. "Let us see if we can find it." He led the way up the street, looking in each shop window as they passed. Finally, he pushed open a door and led the way into a small shop, with little in it except a chair, a counter and a range of decently executed engravings. Thouless turned to Redfern with a triumphant air, as if challenging him to find him wrong, but without saying a word. Redfern had been confused—his friend had never shown any signs of unnatural appetites, and he was sure, himself, that he had given no sign of it outwardly, for he was well practised in his deceit against the world.

The young man that Thouless had run to ground looked patiently and expectantly at the two men. Redfern found that he could not, in all truth, fault his friend for his taste, for the beauty of the shop-keeper—as it seemed that was who he was—was of that androgynous meld so beloved of the aesthete, whilst somehow not leaving the observer with any doubt of his masculinity. His shoulders were nicely broad, and his hands were large but slender, the fingers long and ending with blunt nails. His hair was corn-gold, his eyes wide and set far-apart—they might have been thought to be a fault, perhaps, on some men, but the strength of the nose balanced them, all over-topping generous lips that Redfern knew instantly he wanted to taste.

He pulled himself together, and berated himself. *I'm gawping like a landed trout!* He realised that Thouless was talking to the vision, and quite normally—not staring at him like some shocked choirboy. He tore his eyes away from the young man and managed to catch up on what his friend was saying.

"Sadly, no. My property is in Ireland and what isn't damp is derelict—but Redfern here," Thouless said, indicating his companion with his silver-topped cane, "has a fine townhouse, all new and fancied-up. Ain't that right, Redfern?"

"Er...yes?"

"I was remarking on the fine architectural pictures that Mr. Frost here does." Redfern felt idiotic that somehow he'd missed the introductions. "Good work, what? The detail on Easterby's place here, all those tiles and fluted bits."

"Er, yes." He cursed himself for the seeming inability to say anything, anything at all.

Thouless raised one darkly handsome eyebrow. "Well, then," he said with exquisite patience and the subtlety of a rhinoceros, "*perhaps* Mr. Frost might be persuaded to do a commission, were you not saying that you were thinking of getting some pictures done? Of the house?"

Redfern could feel himself colouring, as for the

third time, and, convinced he looked like some cork-brained nincompoop, all he could find to say was, "Yes. Yes, I was."

Somehow, he'd snapped himself out of his shock, and in moments, the young man—Gideon Frost—had written down Redfern's name and address in, Redfern could not help but notice, an elegant hand, and had promised to call within a few days. He'd explained that his assistant was unwell but he had every hope that his recovery was imminent. Redfern left the shop with a spring in his step he hadn't had for many a month and found it difficult not to smirk. Thouless—*damn his questing eyes*—commented favourably on Frost's talents all the way back to Fleet Street. To cover up his interest in the young man, Redfern said, "Are you trying to shock me, Finn? To hear you speak, I'd think you were quite smitten by young Frost."

Finbarr hailed a hackney, and as it trundled along the street toward them, he said, "I appreciate art, Joshua. That young man creates it, and his Creator has made it in him. If you tell me you did not see the beauty in him, I will call you a bowyer and as such I will never believe anything you say again."

Redfern had grunted something, enough to placate his friend and make him change the subject onto the ball of that night, and that had been the end of the matter between them.

When Frost came to sketch the house, there was no archly sarcastic wag to confuse matters. But it did no good. For all that Redfern wanted to be the charmer, the urbane friend to Frost that Thouless was to him, he found it impossible. He was not so much tongue-tied, but seemingly tongue-*less* in the young man's presence and all he had been able to do was give the engraver carte blanche to sketch where and how he liked. He sounded curt and gruff even to his own ears, and he knew that it was self-protection; better to appear an arrogant nouveau-riche than to give any hint of his true feelings. For from the moment he'd seen Frost again he knew that he was violently, passionately attracted to the young man, in a way that he hadn't felt for many years.

He left Frost to sketch, and forced himself not to trouble his work. He stayed in his library, giving orders to the staff that he had left the house and that he would call on the engraver presently. He sat and wrestled with the burgeoning attraction for the man he'd seen twice. What good would it do to moon after the young man? What good had it ever done? He'd learned harsh lessons in his life, that his predilections had brought nothing but danger and misery to all concerned. He'd long been of the opinion that it was better to live like a monk than to put one more man at risk.

So what, he wondered, as he stood outside Frost's shop on a freezing day, had led his footsteps back here? There was nothing in their business that could not have been done by servants or by correspondence, but here he was. Before he gave it another thought and talked himself out of it, he pushed open the door, and suddenly, as he saw the engraver stand with a welcoming smile on his face, he was warm.

CHAPTER FOUR

ideon hurried forward in what space there was. Redfern seemed to swallow up the space in the shop; his height, his width—both would be more in scale with a battlefield, on the back of an impressive charger—than here. It was one of Gideon's fantasies to imagine Redfern decked out in scarlet and gold. But in the confines of the shop, he was out of place, and Gideon feared that one casual and uncontrolled turn might bring down whole shelves of expensive ink.

"Mr. Redfern, I did not expect you." He thought frantically—had his recent pecuniary problems driven the knowledge of a planned meeting from his mind? He couldn't believe that it had, he could never believe that any distraction would erase any appointment he'd have with this man. It was almost hard to breathe, for it seemed as if the man's presence had sucked the air from the room.

Despite the dusting of snow from Redfern's boots, Gideon felt suddenly warm, particularly around the face and a lot lower down.

He didn't expect a swift answer from Redfern, and he was not disappointed. In their two short meetings, Gideon had learned that Redfern was not, like his friend Mr. Thouless, voluble. Rather the opposite, but Gideon rather liked that. His life had been spent in the company of salesmen, of fakirs and showmen, of politicians and quacks. It was solid, somewhat reassuring to meet a man who took time to think about what he said next, and didn't have a glib answer for everything. His friend Thouless had been quite the opposite of Redfern in this regard, Gideon had been quick to notice.

As usual, Redfern was taciturn, seeming as if the printer's shop was the last place he wanted to be. There was an uncomfortable silence in which Gideon continued to look hopefully at his client, feeling more and more idiotic for the stupid and obsequious smile he knew he was wearing.

Eventually: "Yes. I mean, no. You would not. I was in the area and thought I would see how you were doing. How you were...progressing. On the design."

Trying not to read anything more into his client's words than were there, Gideon answered, "I am nearly done, sir."

"Oh, dash it, Frost, 'sir' makes me sound like I'm in me dotage."

Gideon felt himself colouring. "If you insist, s...Mr. Redfern."

"And I ain't my father, either."

"Indeed." Gideon hardly knew what to say, and the conversation was baffling him. He didn't even know what the man wanted, not that he was complaining, for just to have the opportunity to look at Redfern, awkward silences or not, was like a gift he was not expecting. But however handsome he found the man, he wasn't going to cross the line from tradesman to acquaintance. "I hope you don't want to see the work..."

"Well, I was hoping to."

Gideon stepped in front of the small bench, "It's a matter of habit. Of custom." *Call it superstition and have done, will you?* "I find it has been bad luck to show a client a commission before it's done. You expressed yourself satisfied with the sketches."

"Oh, oh completely. Yes." The big man looked flustered again and Gideon felt a little flutter of panic. Maybe he wanted to cancel the commission? Perhaps it was a question of funds? It wasn't something he could broach. *I should have insisted on a larger deposit.* He couldn't afford to lose money on this work.

"Then? How may I assist you?"

He waited patiently while Redfern seemed to grope for words. "No. That was it, actually."

Gideon had a thought and turned around and rummaged through his papers. When he turned around, he was holding one of the charcoal sketches and he held it out to Redfern. "I am sorry to discommode you. To come all this way just to be disappointed." Redfern seemed embarrassed by

Gideon's words and blustered that, truly, he had been in the vicinity. Gideon doubted it, especially in this weather but he continued to hold the drawing out. "Please, it's not good enough for display, but enough to get an idea of the finished piece. I'd like you to have it."

"Then I will." Gideon watched Redfern looking at the paper. Then the big man pointed to the paper. "You've put me in here. I wasn't even standing there at the time."

Feeling himself colour again, Gideon turned away, abruptly. He hadn't meant to give Redfern that particular sketch. It was fairly obvious to anyone that a great deal more detail had been put into the figure at the gates than had been spent on the house. People might wonder at that, and worse, they might look at the rather hurried work on the house and doubt the artist's skill. "I like to add details to bring a little flavour...I find myself putting things in that aren't there. An artistic foible, if you wish. I assure you, you won't be in the finished piece. Unless you wish it."

"Oh." To Gideon's ears, Redfern sounded a little perturbed. Perhaps he didn't like people to add artistic foibles; some people were put off by art, he knew. Well, it was too late for the engraving. What was done was done. He changed the subject.

"Perhaps your friend Mr. Thouless might be buying property in town?"

"I doubt it," Redfern was frowning and his eyes kept returning to the paper in his hands. "When will you be done?"

"On time," Gideon said. "By the end of next

week." He could easily have finished it in a very few days, but Redfern seemed to have no idea of that. "Let me give you something to carry that in." He pulled a tube from a shelf and moved to take the sketch from Redfern. As he took the awkward thing from the man's hands, his fingers brushed against the back of Redfern's and the man jumped as sharply as if Gideon had grabbed his prick. Their eyes met and Gideon saw something like fear in Redfern's eyes. *Ah, well,* he thought, *better to know now, rather than live in any sort of hope.* He backed away as if nothing had happened, rolled the paper expertly and handed it back to Redfern in the carrying tube.

"No need to collect, of course, sir," he said, dropping carefully into his place as a shopkeeper, as *trade*. "I will bring the framed print around— and the plate—as promised."

He retreated behind his counter, keeping himself under control as Redfern gave a short nod, made a strange guttural noise and swept out of the door. Icy wind flooded the shop, and Gideon let himself relax. He knew he had been stupid— insane to allow himself to harbour feelings for Redfern but he hadn't been able to help himself. He'd rarely met anyone with such vitality, with such presence. Gruff and taciturn he certainly was, but to Gideon it seemed like everything was warmer, more real, more colourful, when he was near.

Just a few more days, he thought as he sat down, picked up his burin and started to work the copper with tiny, delicate movements. *Just a few more days and I'll see him again. Perhaps he'll be so pleased with the work he'll want something else.* Gideon had little hope of that, but he clung to it. It was the only relationship they could have, and Gideon knew it. It wasn't as if he could call on Redfern as if he were an acquaintance. A friend.

When Mord came back, his arms filled with packages, he found his master hard at work and humming tunelessly, a small smile on his handsome face.

And what did that achieve? Redfern berated himself mercilessly as he marched through the narrow streets. *Nothing. Nothing except to make yourself uncomfortable.* His cock was hard, and he was grateful for his redingote which hid a multitude of sins, literally. He cursed himself for not having been able to strike up the simplest of conversations with Frost, and even more so for jumping like a nervous virgin when their skin had touched. It had taken just about every ounce of willpower not to grab Frost's hand and draw him closer—and damn and blast it to hell, he'd *wanted* to. But he knew that would never do; he'd only approached those he'd been sure of, and the surest way to exile and a ruined reputation was to make advances to a man who was likely to reject them.

So he went home, to his newly renovated mausoleum that shouted of his status, but that, in its echoing halls, also whispered of his loneliness. He spent a solitary evening with his fantasies of Gideon Frost, got very drunk and his butler eventually put him into bed, as he'd sacked his valet the day before. The next morning he sat moodily in his breakfast room, staring blankly out of the window, thinking of a certain lieutenant, how good he'd looked in his breeches and gold-frogged coat—and how sordid he must have looked dangling from a rope.

When Mordecai knocked at the shop the next morning, Gideon struggled to open the door. The wood was damp and had frozen to the frame, and it took several shoves before it cracked free. Rubbing a bruised shoulder, Gideon motioned the boy in. Despite having to wait in the cold, his hands tucked under his armpits to keep them warm, the boy's face was wreathed in a broad smile, and once inside the shop he showed no sign of peeling off his clothes.

"It's 'appened, guv, it's frozen solid! Come down and see?" His enthusiasm was hard to ignore, and, infected by it, Gideon decided that the shop could wait for an hour.

"Take your cane," Mord said, dashing to the umbrella rack and grabbing the cane there. "It's proper slippy by the steps."

The two of them made their way through the frozen streets, and despite having to clutch each other several times, and with the support of Gideon's cane, both of them took a tumble or two before they reached the Puddle Dock Stairs. At the top, they paused and Gideon pulled his scarf away from his face to look out across the river.

Snow and ice often made London more attractive than she normally appeared. A deep hoar frost would tinge the old lady with a veil of beauty, and heavy snow—until it was trampled to a brown mush—would clothe the city in a ballgown of shining white.

The river was startlingly bright, and it seemed that the distance between north and south banks had shrunk somehow. In a way, he realised, it had—for now, for a man to cross the river, all he had to do was walk straight across—and not make the detour to Blackfriars or Waterloo. In fact, as they stood and watched, many people were already out on the ice; mostly children and stray dogs, the sounds of their play squealing and screaming eerily as if they were under the arches of the great bridges, but some men too, striding carefully forward, holding sticks before them.

It was some sight, and one he'd not seen in his life before. *No wonder*, he mused, *that Mordecai was so entranced by it. If I were thirteen, I'd be just as excited.*

Gideon realised suddenly that there were men at the bottom of each set of stairs, too, attempting to keep the growing crowds away, which as more and more people arrived and pushed their way down the steps, was proving to be a near impossible task.

"Do you think they'll let us out there?" Mord's ears were bright pink and Gideon pulled the boy's scarf up to cover them.

"When they've made sure it's safe." Gideon didn't think for one moment that anyone would really care if it was safe or not. It would just be an excuse for London to congregate and celebrate something unusual.

A man standing shoulder-to-shoulder with Gideon turned around to the pair of them and said, "Oh, they announced it about half an hour ago, according to that man down there." He tipped his head towards the burly man guarding the base of the steps. "But they won't let the stalls on the ice until they've driven that cart out, to test the weight." He pointed up the river a way where a dray was moving up and down.

"Stalls!" Mordecai's voice was urgent, and excited.

Gideon nodded his thanks at the man. "Come on, Mord, we've wasted enough time."

Mord chattered with excitement all the way back to the shop, and Gideon had to admit that he felt as giddy as the boy. It seemed that word had got around and that Mord and Gideon were walking in the wrong direction. Men laden down with canvas, boxes of books, easels and tables pushed their way southwards towards the river and it didn't take Mord's fevered look to communicate to Gideon that other people thought as the boy did.

As he unlocked the door to the shop he'd made a decision. "Mord," he said, grinning into the boy's anticipatory expression, "go get your brothers and a couple of workmen. We're going to set up shop on the ice."

CHAPTER FIVE

The move was fraught with danger; when Mordecai realised that Gideon intended to move the printing press, he showed some doubt at the enterprise for the very first time. Eight strong men manhandled the press into a cart after Gideon had swiftly removed most of the handles and screws to ease transportation, and slowly they made their way down the slippery ash-strewn streets to the stairs.

Gideon could hardly watch as the men stepped onto the ice for the first time, but after a moment he was assured that no one was going to plummet to an icy death. According to one drunken bystander, an elephant was due to be led across the ice to prove to the populace how safe it was.

"Seems to me they don't need persuadin'," Mord observed as they followed the press down the stairs. "More like that they need keeping off."

Gideon himself felt strangely buoyed up at the

change in routine. "They'll be charging them to come down the stairs any time soon, if I'm any judge. You were the one looking forward to this," he observed, "I'll be the first to admit I'm impressed."

It was surely an impressive sight. From everywhere, hawkers and tradesmen were appearing; victuallers selling food and drink were already in place, as were the street traders: knife grinders, toy-makers, patterers and muffin-men. The stalls were arranged along the length of the river, near the banks, leaving a broad expanse in the centre where, the buying populace of London could already be seen, parading up and down.

Gideon and Mordecai followed the men as they carried the press down the line of stalls and placed it, with imprecations of care from a nervous Gideon, a little back from the main line so that the table could be put in front. Gideon paid the men and then, while Mord went back for more merchandise, arranged what he had on the table. He had seen other larger printing concerns on the ice as they had walked down the lines. Some displayed their presence with huge banners over their stalls and some were even under the cover of large triangular tents. When Mordecai returned, Gideon walked down the main thoroughfare as carefully as he could, for the ice was still not easy to walk on, despite the ash and sawdust strewn in layers underfoot. He visited two of the other printer's tents, passing the time of day with the men he knew before going back to the stall. He gave Mordecai some pennies to get hot drinks for them both and then, blowing on his hands to warm them a little, he started to sketch the scene before him. It was clear that's what the others were doing, and he was determined not to be left behind. Visitors were always eager to buy anything colourful, even garish, that was a memento of something unusual.

They did well on the first day, although it was a cold and miserable place to be sitting trading. They spent more on sliced hot meat and warming drinks than ever they would have done in the shop, but they made three times as much in sales, and on the next day, this improved again—for Gideon toiled through most of the night to get the small engraving of the Frost Fair completed. It could not compare with the size and the multi-coloured garish prints that some of the others were producing, but it was detailed and crisp, and most importantly had the date on it, which would commemorate the event. Customers told Gideon that they could almost see the movement within it, and the steam rising from the shoppers' breath. For his own part, Gideon was sure that it was the cold of the day and the steam rising from their own breaths that was convincing, but he always thanked the customers, and took their money with a smile.

It sold well, and Mordecai was keeping as busy as ever he had been before, between helping Gideon print more copies and serving the customers. His small round face was pale but pink-cheeked as he extolled their luck, and that of his mother, whose fish-cart was doing a roaring trade at the other end of the icy thoroughfare, now dubbed "Freezeland Street".

It was with chilled hands but a light heart that Gideon was wrestling with a jammed screw on the third day, his coat off as he sweated in exertion, when he heard a voice he recognised.

"Your representation is rather picturesque and, if you don't mind me saying, Mr. Frost, rather a misrepresentation. The ice now; that I can see, is lumpy and—frankly—strewn with the filth of London, whereas you make it look like a millpond, pristine and white. Why represent it thus?"

Gideon turned around, the sweat sticking coldly to his back, and he pulled on his coat and overcoat before he froze. The man he remembered being with Redfern on their first acquaintance was holding one of the printed views in an elegant black glove. Gideon suddenly found he couldn't remember the gentleman's name and felt a blush creep up his cheeks.

"It's what will be remembered, sir," he said. "I find that if I'm asked for a picture then my customer is more impressed if he has a pleasing representation. The scene you see may be, in all actuality, covered in rags and rubbish, the snow may be trampled and ruined, but in a few years that's not what people will see, in here." He tapped his head, wondering as he did, why he'd bothered with such a lengthy explanation.

A few gentlemen, as elegantly and as foppishly clad as Mr. Redfern's friend gathered around, and

Gideon realised they must be his companions.
Damn it, he thought angrily, *why can't I remember the man's name?* "Sir" was safe, but a little
embarrassing.

"You are probably right," the gentleman said,
with a smile that had something not quite right
about it, "I'm sure Redfern is immensely impressed with his...what did you call it? Ah yes—
his *pleasing representation.*"

"I'm sure I don't know—"

"Why the sketch you did of him, of course."

"You mean of the house, sir. The house." Gideon felt wrong-footed, as if he'd done something
wrong, angry at himself for having given Redfern
the wrong sketch and galled that the man had
shown it—shown it off, by the sounds of things—
to his friends.

"Of course," the gentleman said, with that
same sly smile. "The house, how careless of me."
The two gentlemen at the man's side were smiling
as if in on the joke and Gideon felt a slow burning
anger that they could tease him so. "Forgive me.
And let me repair the damage I've done, will you?"

"No harm taken, sir, believe me."

"If you say so, it is generous of you. My Irish
mouth does run on, what? Let me make amends
anyway. Do you do portraits on commission all? I
don't remember seeing any in your shop."

"I don't as a rule, sir."

"Oh, why ever not, man? You've obviously a
talent for it. I don't mean an engraving, damn me.
I'd look fair ghastly with all those lines and scrib-
bles. I'd want something to mount." The man was

smiling still, but it was more normal. However one of his friends had a sudden coughing fit and had to be slapped hard on the back by the others.

"I don't paint, sir," Gideon said.

"I'm sure you could."

Gideon could, but his work never pleased him. To think of selling second-class wares made him shy from it. "I don't, sir. I'm sorry. But I could do a silhouette, if that suited you? If you'll wait a moment..." He turned to the back of the stall and rummaged through a box of older prints that he hadn't considered in good enough condition to sell but he had found that if he inked "*Bought on the River Thames*" on them, together with the date, people would buy anything. He pulled a framed silhouette out, a commission he'd done a year or so back and had never been paid for. It was of a rather rotund gentleman in front of a night scene of trees and a ruined castle, the background all done in black and white chalks. "Something like this—it's not my best work, but..."

"Rather say that it's not your best subject," the man said. "Heavens, what a sight. I trust you'd flatter me a little, make a pleasing representation?" He was teasing again, but Gideon was a little more used to it.

"Of course, sir. If that's what you'd like."

"Zounds!" The man turned to his friends. "The printer don't win customers by his flattery in the least!" His friends laughed dutifully. He reached into his pocket, retrieving a small gold card case that made Mordecai gasp. "Here. My card. Come tonight, for tomorrow I'm likely to be called away and may be back to Ireland for a month at least. We can arrange terms when you come." He dropped a card onto the table.

"At what time should I call, Mr. Thouless?" Gideon read the card in time to save himself.

Now he'd got what he wanted, the man almost seemed to have lost interest and was moving away. "Oh, I don't suppose it matters much. Seven o clock?"

Gideon nodded, gave a short bow in appreciation of the patronage and the commission, and, while Mordecai sold a man a framed view of Brighton, watched the small group walk away, jealous of their exquisitely tailored clothes, their expensive silken hats. The men stopped at the next stall, an apothecary, and one of Thouless' companions turned and was looking back at Gideon with a small frown on his face as if he was trying to remember who he was. Gideon paled and he felt the strength seep from his legs. The man, now arm in arm with Thouless and walking away with him, chatting conspiratorially, was none other than the young man Gideon had met in St Paul's Churchyard not a week ago.

CHAPTER SIX

"Gid. *Gid*? Gideon!" The voice seemed to come from far away and it took Mord to pull him back to the moment. The boy jabbed his elbow into him to attract his attention. Gideon turned and found Mord gesturing behind with him a frown.

"'E's gone round the back."

Gideon stepped carefully across the sacking and layer of straw he'd put down to keep a sure footing, and around the back of the press he found the smiling face of his friend, Duncan Verney. Short, round, and with a cheerful face, Duncan ran a gang of chimney sweeps to the eternal shame of his family, printers all, who had wanted Duncan to follow in their footsteps. It galled them that Duncan had taken to such a filthy trade, and more so that he was getting rich at it.

Gideon smiled but knew that it was a little distracted, knew also too well what his friend would want. "Duncan. Not exactly where I would imagine I would see you."

"No." The man grinned. "Not exactly the best place to sell my wares, is it?" He gave a knowing look to the group of gentlemen on the next stall, "But I've got a boy giving out some of the leaflets you did for me in the summer. You're doing all right, though?"

"Surprisingly. It's well worth almost freezing to death for. It might keep the wolf from the door a little longer."

"Come and have something to eat," Duncan said.

"I can't, Duncan, you've seen how busy we are."

"Oh, come on. Your boy can manage the stall for an hour, can't you, boy?"

Mordecai glared at the sweep, but gave Gideon a haughty reassurance, and drew himself up to his true height, which wasn't much. Gideon had to suppress a smile. "I can manage, guv. We got enough prints for now. Ain't going to sell them all this morning. We can print more when you comes back. Anything more unusual, I can takes orders like in the shop. Go on." Gideon hesitated a moment longer, and Mord added, "Wouldn't mind a pie or two though, when you come back."

"Come on then, man," Duncan said. "Before my balls freeze off."

The crowds were thicker on the ice than they had been the day before and it took a while to wend their way back to the embankment and up into the city streets. It was a short step to Walker's Hotel by Blackfriars and it wasn't until

Gideon had a glass of ale in one hand and a pot of coffee to warm his fingers on that he finally felt he was thawing out. As Duncan poured them both some coffee, Gideon took the opportunity to observe him. It has been a few months since he'd last seen him, and no doubt the hard weather had done nothing to reduce his success in his chosen trade. All available fireplaces would be opened up, cleaned and in action in weather like this. One couldn't tell by Duncan's appearance, though, for he wore his oldest clothes whilst working, which were tattered and frayed. His cuffs invisible, his hat patched, but all were surprisingly clean, considering his profession. But he didn't go up the chimneys much these days, Gideon reflected.

He let himself relax. It was good to let someone else pay for a change. He knew Duncan well enough not to suggest anything else, and he knew that Duncan knew exactly what kind of financial straits he was in. How he always seemed to know this, Gideon couldn't tell; it was something they rarely spoke of, but the sweep always seemed to know whether Gideon's finances were afloat, or going down for the second time.

"It's good to see you, Duncan," he said.

Two large and steaming pies were delivered to the table and there was silence for minutes as immediate cold and hunger were pushed to one side. Eventually Duncan sat back a little and drained his glass. "You too. I wish I'd been around more but—busy time, you know?"

"I can imagine," Gideon said. "Your family?"

"Forget it. There's no hope there. I have soiled

my hands and my reputation. I'm a gypsy. In fact, I'm a shit-sack, according to my father's last correspondence."

"He can't keep it up forever."

"He will; you underestimate him. He called me a slaver. I don't own my boys, you know that."

Gideon grimaced. Chimneys had to be swept and they weren't big things. Small boys were the right size for the work. Any successful sweep had at least a boy or two working for him, and Duncan had ten, at least at the last count. "Be patient," Gideon said, "he'll forgive you. He'll have to." Duncan was the only son.

"Not he. He's getting married again. Plans to replace me completely. Ah, forget it, Gid. You know that's not why I'm here. You all right?"

Gideon gave half a laugh. *No*, he wanted to say—*do you think I'd be freezing my arse off on the river if things were all right? I have one decent commission and I'm undercharging for that because I'm in love with my client and if he doesn't pay...* "You never change, Duncan. I'm fine. Truly. I'm still employing Mord. The day I can't afford to pay his wage is the day you need to worry about me. I've told you that before."

Reapplying himself to the beefsteak pie, Duncan sounded relieved. "All right. But you'd let me know? You're the only one who—well... You know. Was there. I owe you a lot."

"You owe me nothing. A bed and a few meals while you found work? It took you no time at all. You've bought me more meals on the strength of two week's hospitality than I was ever owed." The conversation always went this way, and Gideon hated it. Hated that Duncan was so generous and hated that he was never in a position to reciprocate. "Just shut up and let me enjoy my pie."

Duncan complied and they finished their meal with little more than small talk and discussion of Gideon's commission. The sweep knew little of art, but was happy to listen. If he picked up on Gideon's interest in Redfern he gave no sign of it. However, when the meal ended, Duncan leant across the table, and spoke in a low urgent tone, using the hubbub of the hotel to mask his words. "Gid. Why don't we get a room?"

His heart sank. He had had an inkling that this had been coming. There had been something pent-up about his friend today and he should have recognised the signs more clearly. They'd experimented physically at school, finding that they both enjoyed it, and once or twice since, they'd tumbled into bed together. But it was nothing regular, nothing structured. Fumbles in the dark when no one was looking, cold hands on warm cocks in a hired carriage, and one long night in Duncan's bed when his parents were out at the theatre. But they'd been little more than boys then. They weren't those boys anymore.

After his parents disowned him and Duncan had moved into the little printer's shop, Duncan had attempted to rekindle their relationship but Gideon had put him off. And he'd been putting him off ever since.

"I can't, Duncan."

"Oh come on. Just for an hour or two? Mord

won't miss you."

With a sigh, Gideon pushed his chair back. Everything came with a price, it seemed. Even friendship. "I'm sorry," he said. He genuinely was. "But it's too dangerous and Mord's on his own." It hurt him to see the rejection flash in his friend's eyes. "I'm sorry."

A silence stretched between them, a silence in which Gideon imagined he could see their friendship shattering like too-thin ice. It was becoming hard to continue to look his friend in the face, until Duncan sighed and smiled an almost normal smile. "Can't blame me, can you?"

The atmosphere seemed to click back to normal, like the smooth drop of the printing press. "I could, but I know how weak-willed you are," laughed Gideon. "Perhaps I should have said yes. I don't want to be responsible for you finding your guttersnipes suddenly irresistible."

Duncan made a face and looked utterly revolted. "There are times, Mr. Frost, when I wonder why I even keep your friendship."

"Me too," said Gideon, happy that he'd sidestepped the invitation once again.

"So, are you going to tell me about the devastating pair of Irish eyes who was being most agreeable to you this morning?"

"No, I'm not. He's a prospective client."

"Gone upmarket from the Churchyard, haven't you?"

Gideon kicked him under the table. "Are you trying to get me arrested?"

"Sorry, Gid." Duncan looked suitably abashed,

but Gideon was angry again. He had sold himself no more than ten times in his life and somehow everything seemed to rotate around sex and money. Even his best friend didn't see how insulting it was to refer to his whoring. *I'm not a whore,* he thought furiously. *I'm practical. Independent. Not a whore.*

He stood up, and pulled a coin purse from his pocket. Duncan started to remonstrate, seeing how he'd offended his friend but it was too late. Gideon threw enough coins on the table to cover his meal and for the pie he was taking back for Mord and walked out without another word. Duncan caught up with him at the corner of Earl Street and pulled him into an alley. His breath streamed into the enclosed space like a dragon's, and his face was white with worry.

"Look, Gid. I don't know what I said—but I'm sorry. Every time we meet you end up walking out on me. I promise I won't ask you for—a favour, you know. Again. I miss you, Gid. That's all."

At first, Gideon tried to pull his arm from Duncan's grip, but the sweep was strong and his penitence was real. He sighed. "You're my friend. I don't want us to be more than that. It means too much to me, do you understand?"

"No," said Duncan, "I don't. But I respect you, Gid, even if I don't understand you, and I understand you even less every time we meet. You won't take my money. You won't come in with the business. You won't take anything else from me. What do you want?"

"Nothing. Nothing. I'm sorry you can't understand that."

The sweep threw up his soot-ingrained hands. "I don't have to understand you to like you. So, all's snug between us? Still friends?"

Gideon led the way out of the alley. "Of course, you blasted lily-white. You really are an idiot. I blame your infantile behaviour on the age of your workers. You should mix with older people from time to time."

"Now you mention it, you could assuage my broken-hearted rejection..." Duncan thumped him on the arm, "...with the name of your fine Irish benefactor."

"Who is buying a silhouette," Gideon said firmly. "Nothing more."

"Did I say anything to the contrary? But I'll wager he has a house with a lot of chimneys."

They'd reached the top of the stairs and Gideon turned and shook Duncan's hand. He didn't object when Duncan slipped the price of the meal back into his hand. "Oh yes, that will encourage the man to buy my work when I point out how sooty his house is, and that I number lily-whites amongst my bosom acquaintance." He laughed, "All right, I'll see what I can do. No promises."

"You're a gent," Duncan said, dropping into the street accent he used as a professional sweep and turning away.

"So are you, in case you forget," he called out after his friend, who raised his hand in acknowledgement, and disappeared into the throng. He gave a deep sigh as he warmed his fingers on Mord's pie and set off down the steps to the river.

He cared a lot for Duncan, and he knew Duncan felt the same way, but it wasn't enough. He knew that Duncan was lonely; he could hardly be anything else working out of his class the way he did, and Gideon had to admit that he was lonely too. But as fun as sex with Duncan had been when they were younger—and it had been a great deal of fun, the sort of fun two men could have when they knew each other's likes as well as they did—it wasn't enough for either of them. And it wasn't fair to Duncan to let him think otherwise.

Redfern put his feet up on the stool and felt the heat of the roaring fire through his leather soles. His luncheon sat heavily under his waistband and he was supremely comfortable. "I'm not damned surprised you're chilled through, Finn." Thouless stood close by, back to the fire, warming his balls. "Whatever possessed you? You won't find me slipping around on the ice and waiting to drop through. No matter how fashionable the river has become."

"Immensely fashionable, unfortunately. One don't have the boots to cope with the conditions. Oh, and I saw your pretty printer down there, you might like to know..."

Redfern sat up sharply, his boots hitting the floor with a thump. His friend raised an eyebrow at him, and Redfern cursed himself for showing his feelings. "Ah. Frost was down on the ice?"

"Printing presses spring from the ice like mushrooms on shit. Your Galahad was there with all the others who...salesmen." He stretched. "I'd almost forgotten about it, actually. After that someone fell through the ice. It was terribly exciting."

"Not for the poor soul who fell through."

"I believe it was only some urchin. Didn't put many people off."

"Someone's child, damn it."

"I doubt it," Thouless said. "No one seemed to know whose it was. It didn't come back up, anyway."

Redfern frowned at his friend's callous description of the child's death. "I don't care much to parade myself in the freezing cold just in the hope that I might see another poor child die. Ghouls, people are. Nothing but ghouls."

"That's your trouble," Thouless replied. "You don't care for fashion. You don't have to bow and scrape to society to be accepted. You aren't on the fringe."

"And neither would you be if you played their games to the end instead of taking one step forward and three steps back. You attend their functions, you toady with the best of them and then you go and scandalise your hostess by taking her daughter into the garden—or persuading her to meet with you in some damnable coffee house."

Thouless raised an eyebrow and looked down at his friend. "You are très knowledgeable considering the last function you went to was to celebrate the launch of the ark."

"A vile calumny," Redfern said, waving his hand at the footman who filled their glasses. "It was for Salome's dance. And I may not step out in the depths of the *ton*, but I hear things all the same."

"Your dear brother."

Redfern looked up sharply, "Finn, I've warned you. Leave the boy alone—he's no match—and certainly no threat to you."

Thouless met Redfern's challenging glance for a moment, then dissolved into a charming smile. "Ah, Joshua, I wouldn't harm a hair on his head. Can't imagine what the boy has against me. Well, I can't stay, I have guests expected—and a most delightful one to add to the mix, if my invitation is accepted."

Redfern pulled the rope for the footman and walked his friend to the door. "It's about time you stopped breaking hearts, Finn, and settled down."

"You know, I was thinking the very same thing myself." Thouless shrugged on his coat and left the house, leaving Redfern with a smile on his face at his friend's uncaring attitude to the good graces of society.

He sat quietly for a while, thinking over what Thouless had said, and then stood with a bounce. "Why not?" he said to the empty room. "Why shouldn't I go down there? Half of London is on the ice, so why not I?" He rang for his man and ordered a cab.

Stupid, he berated himself as he confronted the press of people coming up and down the stairs to the river. *How stupid. The least I could have done was to ask Thouless where his stall was.* But something had made him uncomfortable in doing that, and it wasn't something he could quantify.

For all Thouless' dandy-like mannerisms, he was a ladies' man, and Redfern liked the man's friendship, damn it. He set off down the steps and joined the throng moving eastwards.

It took him half an hour to find Frost. Other printers had more of an obvious presence. Flags, banners and pictures hung around their stalls, proclaiming their art and their wares. Frost's temporary shop was no more than a table. It seemed, though, as Redfern approached, that the celebratory spirit of London extended to everyone and they were prepared to buy from every tradesman, even if they weren't making as large a display as their colleagues. There were several people around Frost's table, most of them buying a small but nicely detailed print of the Fair itself.

"I don't like the feel of the ice," Frost was saying to his assistant after he thanked the last customer for his purchase. "I think we should pack it up tonight."

His assistant seemed to be more practical. "Just one more day, guv," he said. "The boatman said it's safe enough."

"It wasn't for that poor child, and a child weighs a lot less...Oh!" Frost had seen him, and moved forwards to the table. "Mr. Redfern! What a pleasure. How may I help you?"

Joshua found he was smiling like a fool, and to his intense pleasure and a slight tightening of his trousers, he was absurdly happy that Frost was smiling back. Not the humble yet obsequious smile of a shopkeeper for a customer, or even the smile of a craftsman who owed his client a commission, but a wide, open grin of a man who was genuinely pleased to see someone. Perhaps a friend.

"I was—" He searched for a lie, and cursed himself for not having one ready. Damn it, he'd had plenty of time. "I had heard my friends were here, and thought I would surprise them. Imagine how pleased I was to be surprised to find you. Are you not freezing?"

Frost's face gave a wry smirk, and his assistant rolled his eyes as if to underline the stupidity of the remark, then blushed crimson when he saw that Redfern had noticed.

Redfern wanted to say something else, but everything seemed too personal, and couldn't be said at all—let alone here in the open. He wanted to say that Gideon's coat was too thin for the elements, that he'd love to buy him a better one. He wanted to say that Gideon looked paler than last week, that he seemed thinner and the blue shadows under his eyes were probably caused by working too hard. But of course he couldn't say anything like that.

"The, er...commission?"

"On time, sir. I promised you it would be done by Friday and on Friday it will be. I think you'll be pleased with it."

Redfern nodded. It wasn't the conversation he wanted to have, and the longer he stood there, the more obvious it was that he didn't have anything useful to say. The silence became more and more awkward and Redfern was forced to rummage through the prints of the Fair. "I'll take a few of these," he said, helplessly. Then, as Frost took them from him to wrap, he was finally struck by inspiration. "Look, Frost. I've been meaning to ask you this before now, but Th...others said that I should wait until I saw your completed piece. I hardly think that's necessary, do you?"

Complete incomprehension showed on the young man's face. "I don't know, sir—" he said carefully, as if expecting something to explode. "It depends."

"Well, yes of course," Redfern said, irritated with himself being unable to cut to the nub of the conversation, but improvisation was not his forte. "I have a house in the country, and, well, as you...Oh dash it. It's too bloody cold to stand here and discuss it. Surely we can talk in the warm, at least."

He was rewarded by Frost colouring this time, and the colour suited him well; he really was too damned pale, damn it. "I'm afraid..."

Redfern felt possessed by some muse. "Don't be afraid, man. Just let's get out of this cold and I'll tell you what I need done."

"Go on, guv," the small assistant said. Redfern noticed that he had a thicker coat on than Frost, and a large fur hat, whereas Frost's hat would keep no one warm. "It's getting dark now, anyhow. I'll start packing up and when you come back, we'll go home. Can't rely on this lark for more than another day."

Frost was still hesitating, so Redfern seized the advantage. "I won't hear another word," and grabbed the surprised man by the arm and hauled him out. Frost's forearm, even under his coat, was so slim that it shocked Redfern. Was the man even eating enough to stay alive, or was he spending it all on that blasted printing press and getting nothing back?

Seated across from the printer in a small, dark coffee house, Redfern studied Gideon closely. The young man had the smallest of frowns on his face and his hands, now free of their cheap gloves, were clasped together around the dish of Turkish. He looked distinctly uncomfortable, and now Redfern had the luxury of examining him at close quarters he could see that he wore clothes that were once of an excellent quality but were stretched, a little too small, darned and patched.

Frost caught his glance and blushed, a reflex that suited him and gave Redfern a frisson of pleasure. However, Frost's expression darkened, no doubt objecting to the kidnap and close critical scrutiny. "I came as requested, sir," he said, and Redfern's heart sank at the formality in his tone, feeling hopeless that he could ever breach the lines between them. "If you would discuss business, I wish that you would. I like not to leave my assistant on the ice on his own, especially as there have been more cracks reported."

"You should take the press off the ice tonight," Redfern said, suddenly full of fear and remembering the callous story that Finn had given him of the child who never came back.

Frost shook his head. "It's too late tonight to arrange for its removal. But I think, tomorrow..." He looked up at Redfern, as if betrayed into discussing matters that he considered were not business of his customer, and Redfern wondered why Frost was so...frosty—there was no other word for it—and what had made him so difficult to approach. "This isn't why you asked me here, sir. "

"My name is Joshua. I've told you that you make me feel old."

"That's inappropriate," Frost said quickly, but Redfern felt something leap inside him as the young man missed off the form of address completely. Could this mean that he wanted to bridge the gap between them?

"Then if you can't call me Joshua, then at least drop the sir and call me Redfern. It's a compromise...Gideon?" Redfern smiled over his coffee cup, wondering what on earth had got into him that he was taking control of the situation like this. When he'd been wooing Lieutenant Neil Pearson (and that was the only word he could use to describe the way he'd pursued the handsome lieutenant), he'd been as shy as he ever was, but he'd found little gifts did much to break the ice. Once his attentions were understood, accepted and reciprocated, Neil had been the admiral of their affair. It was Neil who—during the brief peace in 1802—suggested that he move in with Redfern as a companion, and it was Neil who organised every facet of their liaison after that. He'd been so discreet, so careful to hide their relationship from the outside world that Redfern had been horrified—in 1805 after he'd gone back to sea—when Neil had been court-martialled and hanged for sodomy.

In their brief time together, he'd never once dragged Neil off for an assignation, however innocent. Not in the way he'd just done with Frost. Now here he was insisting that young Frost call him by a more intimate name. *I'm putting him at risk, and I swore I'd never do that again.*

For a moment, Frost seemed to be struggling with himself. Then, losing the battle, he visibly relaxed in the chair, tipped his face up, and met Redfern's eyes. The cold and suspicious, almost fearful look the printer had been wearing melted away like ice around the fire, and for the first time Joshua was treated to the full beauty of Gideon's natural smile. It seemed to Redfern that the sun, now almost gone in the chill winter's evening, had pulled itself up from its western bed and blazed for a long last second in a dingy coffee house in Blackfriars.

"I think that might be acceptable...Redfern."

Redfern had to stop himself from reaching across the table and clasping Gideon's hand. Instead he beamed like the love-struck idiot he was, and ordered more coffee over Frost's insistence that he couldn't stay more than a few minutes longer.

⚬⚭⚬⚭⚬

The local church bell was striking the three-quarters as Thouless surveyed his dining room with a sense of great satisfaction. The candles were of a number that the room was lit with sufficient brightness—one could not say that it was suspiciously dark, but it was not as illuminated as if he were expecting young ladies and their ma-

mas to dine with him, where all must be...circumspect. The table was set for six, although there were, in fact, no guests expected at all. Crystal gleamed golden in the reflected candlelight and even the silverware took on an aureate and therefore mendacious air.

His man had instructions not to enter the room under any circumstances unless summoned. Thouless paid his butler a great deal of money to remain discreet, and therefore continuously employed with a glowing character.

Thouless stood by the fireplace, arranging himself for the best effect for his guest to see when he entered. The thought of the beautiful young printer quite stirred his blood; he was a lover of beautiful things, and the sex of his conquests was never as important as their outward appearances. Plus, he thought petulantly as the clock ticked the time away, Redfern was clearly infatuated. Thouless prided himself that whilst the *ton* might be occasionally scandalised by his flirtations with the weaker sex, they had no inkling that his tastes were far more catholic than they assumed. People were easy to fool. Society. Mammas. Even Redfern, who was the nearest thing he had to a friend in this city, was duped by an effulgence of charm and a propensity for flirting. *Do what they expect of you, and they won't expect the unexpected.*

He heard footsteps on the tiled floor of the hall and his man opened the door. "Mr. Frost, sir," he announced, then left.

Thouless allowed himself one long look at

Frost as he stood by the door. The young man's hair was unruly, and the curls around his forehead were delightfully flattened a little from the hat he'd left in the hall. But the eyes were as beguiling as ever and the lips...Thouless burned at the thought that he could, no—he *would*—would taste those lips before Redfern. Perhaps, if things went as planned, Redfern would never get to taste them at all. His eyes travelled lazily down Frost's lean—too lean for his size—body. There were more things than lips to be tasted, too, Thouless was quite certain of that, and they would be sweet.

"Mr. Frost, how beautifully punctual you are." He offered his hand and got a thrill of pleasure from Frost's cool palm.

"It creates a good impression, sir," Frost said, "at least I hope so." His eyes swept around the room; clearly he had not expected to be received in the dining room. Thouless watched him take in the hellebores and dried white lavender arranged with frosted fruits in a winter centerpiece upon the table. "I, er— I interrupt you, sir." He seemed to notice Thouless' finery, his satin embroidered waistcoat and pale cream pantaloons for the first time. "Perhaps I should come again tomorrow."

"Actually, you catch me rather embarrassed, Mr. Frost." He waved a hand at the table with what he hoped was a crestfallen gesture. "I have been repulsed by my friends for other more exciting amusements. Apparently there is gaming on the ice and my poor table has lost its allure." There was a glimmer of truth in this, too. His friends were gaming on the ice, but the dinner party that appeared to have been deserted was never planned. In his native Ireland, Thouless had worked for a while with a theatre company in Dublin. He'd learned there the value of a set stage. "So, in truth, I am pleased with the diversion. My so-called friends may enjoy freezing in a tent on a surface which may swallow them whole, but I prefer my comfort."

Frost still looked a little rigid; *poised*, Thouless thought fancifully to himself, *like a deer about to fly into the forest.* "Please, Mr. Frost. You'd make me very happy and would be doing me a great favour if you would help me out? Stand in for my missing guests?" He took a step forward and the smile slid from his face as the young man took a sharp step back.

"No," he said, and his face seemed to be a canvas to Thouless' sharp eyes as several expressions flitted over it. Confusion tinged with something else? Fear? A sense of being trapped? "No. No, thank you, sir."

"All right, although my chef will never forgive me. He's been working for days. However," he swept forward and poured a drink and held it out in front of him, "I won't take no for an answer in this."

Frost didn't move, but neither did Thouless. He stood immobile, holding the glass out until Frost gave in, as Thouless knew well he would. "Good man. Now, then. To business." He sat at the table and gestured Gideon to sit beside him, noting the man's obvious reluctance and then gradual acceptance. He was aroused as much by the chase itself as by the pleasure of beating Redfern to Frost's rather obvious charms.

Frost laid a leather satchel on the table, and, as Thouless noted with some delight, hands that were shaking slightly—proving him to be not quite the self-assured young man that he posed to be—and pulled out a handful of silhouettes. "These are not the finest work I have done," he said, handing some over to Thouless, "except I was rather pleased with the effect here, for this gentleman—the detail of the lace was particularly time consuming."

Thouless took his time, both in receiving and returning each sample (which, he thought were singularly dull, as they all appeared to be rotund gentlemen complete with hats and canes) and managed to brush his fingers against Frost's hand with each exchange. He was hard now, and his pantaloons were feeling a little tight under the strain. *Patience was never my suit*, he thought. *God blast virgins*.

"Yes, yes—quite impressive—the devil's in the details, I'm sure. Are you sure I can't persuade you to dine?"

Frost's face registered a touch of suspicion. "I feel, perhaps, sir, that I should leave you these, and you can let me know which style you prefer." He moved to put the portraits back into a neat pile.

Thouless wanted to pounce right there but it was too soon, the young man was not quite re-laxed as yet. How much work was required to break down those walls of ice?

"Forgive me; it's just that I hate to dine alone. And...well, I attempt never to do so, since my wife died." He looked away and down, but not before he saw Frost's face clear and a look of shock and pity take the place of the frown. "It's been three years now, and I still see her, like a spectre, at every meal I have."

"I'm sorry, sir," Frost said, and his voice seemed truly penitent. "I know what it is to lose someone dear, and to know that their absence can never be filled."

"Thank you," Thouless said, and he reached across and took Gideon's hand in both of his. "It's kind of you to care. You'll stay then?" He was gratified when Frost gave a small nod. He let his hand go with some reluctance and summoned his man, giving instructions for the meal.

As they dined, Thouless continued his gentle onslaught, with rising anticipation and frustration. He insisted that Frost sit by his side, not at the end of the table and in such a position that he could touch him on the arm from time to time in the course of conversation. By the end of the meal, Frost had a slightly glazed expression, eased along by Thouless' constant refilling of his glass and the potency of the particular brand of claret. Thouless gauged that the time had come, and, as he touched Frost's arm, one more time his fingers tightened around it, noting with pleasure its delicacy and yet—as Frost pulled back and stood up, knocking his chair over as he did—a strength that belied its appearance.

"Come now, man," Thouless said, excitement fluttering through him. "Did you really think that I'd invite you to my house for such frippery? Surely your victims are easily sketched in your dingy little shop? I know why you came here, and it wasn't for your art, or you'd have never sat at table." He was a few inches taller than Frost and outweighed him by a good twenty pounds; his grip was vice-like and his strength built from hard hunting over his Irish estates.

"Let me go, sir." It amused Thouless enormously that even under duress, the shopkeeper in Frost prevailed. Thouless had hoped that he might have turned on him and spat like a wildcat. His politeness was all so horribly trade. "I misunderstand..."

"You misunderstand nothing," Thouless said, quietly and firmly. "You fired your beauty at Redfern, and while the man is clearly besotted over you, you lost patience with his pathetic inability to speak up and tell you. So you thought you'd try fresh prey, did you? Move your operation from Lad Lane to Mayfair?" He pulled Frost closer, forcing his arm behind his back with practised ease. The printer had gone white and wide-eyed at the mention of Lad Lane. "Oh yes, young Eltham told me where he knew you from. So stop struggling and listen to me."

For a moment, Frost stopped, his face furious but his eyes full of fear. It was delicious to watch. Now for the kill and the final moments of victory.

"All I need do is to tell Redfern. One word from me—and he listens quite intently to my advice—and your precious commission will be no more and he'll no doubt make sure that none of his friends seek you out.

"However," he languidly leant forward and kissed Frost on the neck, licking at his skin and chuckling as Frost squirmed, unable to escape, "I could ensure your prosperity. I could praise your work beyond Redfern's small set. He rarely goes into society, and I am the darling of the *ton* right now. Just imagine what I could do for you." He moved his mouth up to Frost's ear and attempted to reach his lips. "And the price? Is nothing you haven't done for shillings. I could offer you much more than shillings, Gideon. I could make you a very rich man."

He was so busy with his own congratulations, knowing that Frost had no choice but to capitulate, that he missed the fact that Frost had his head turned as far away as he could. With a shout of anger, the young man whipped his head around, and smashed it into Thouless' chin, making him take a sharp step backwards. He lost his footing on the fireguard and he crashed to the floor, pulling Frost down on top of him. Frost was faster to recover and was up and to the door before Thouless had recovered his feet, his ears ringing from the blow to the head.

Thouless lunged toward the door but Frost had it opened—curse his own short-sightedness for not locking it—and had fled into the hall where it was impossible for Thouless to follow without making himself look foolish. He slammed the door shut, then, going to the table, he swept Frost's silhouettes to the floor, followed by the crystal and china, which shattered under his boots like his well-laid plans.

CHAPTER SEVEN

H e was almost all the way home before he realised he'd left, not only his sample silhouettes but also his portfolio at the snake's house. *Snake.* That described Thouless perfectly. Lying hidden and innocent in the grass, then striking with speed and poisoning its victim. Gideon had never actually seen a snake, but now he knew he would never be able to think of Thouless as anything else. He was furious. Angry with Thouless, but angrier with himself for not anticipating that something like this would happen one day. For not realising that the "nice young man" from St Paul's had betrayed him, and for not seeing the trap that Thouless wanted to set. *Had set*, he thought desperately. He may as well have dropped to his knees on the snake's parquet floor, because if Thouless went through with his threat, and Gideon could see no reason on earth why he would not, he might end up whoring full-time, for he would lose everything but passing trade.

And Redfern. If Thouless lied with every breath, how could he believe him when he'd said, *You fired your beauty at Redfern, and while the man is clearly besotted over you...* Could that possibly be true? Or was it just more viciousness from a man who wanted to hurt, and to despoil anything he touched? He wanted beyond anything to believe that it was true, that Redfern truly felt the same way—had the same longings for him... *Joshua.* But he could trust nothing Thouless said or did. It could easily be something he said to encourage Gideon to behave inappropriately—and he knew where he'd end up then. The Pillory. And Newgate. And that was if he was lucky. No. He pushed aside the temptation of believing the snake. He'd do nothing to put Joshua in danger, and he was more than aware of the threat to his own safety, too.

Back at the shop he sat on his bed and tried not to panic over Thouless' extortion. What could he do to prevent Redfern finding out? Nothing, he realised with a sinking heart. Nothing. Redfern would know he was a whore and that would be that. It was unbearable. What would happen after that seemed too immense to contemplate—but even though his future as a printer lay perilously in Thouless' vile palm, the thought of never again seeing Redfern—*Joshua*—cut deep. It seemed easier to imagine and much more imminent than watching his already dwindling trade fail completely. After all, he thought sourly, perhaps he was laying too much hope in Joshua's commission—perhaps Thouless was only cutting the throat of a business that was expiring of a terminal wasting disease.

All he could do was to go to Joshua as soon as he'd taken the cash box down to Mordecai. Just thinking of his assistant caused a further pang of fear. The boy had dragged himself up from the slums—he had turned up in the shop one day, full of confidence and cheek, and had somehow convinced Gideon to give him a week's unpaid trial—and had been a godsend, for companionship, morale boosting and help around the shop. He went to bed, shivering in the chill of the little bedroom and lay awake for hours, finally falling asleep but only escaping to dreams populated by a leering, triumphant Thouless chasing him across a landscape of scattered parchment.

In the morning he had three blissful seconds where the day before was a blank. Then the dining table, the pain of being captured, the extortion, Thouless' handsome, leering face—it all came flooding back, wiping away the nightmares of the night and replacing them with bad dreams of the day. He groaned, and crawled out of bed, wrapping a blanket around him and teasing the fire back into life.

Once dressed he carefully took the plate of Joshua's commission from its drawer and examined it with a critical eye. It was finished. There was only one thing to do with it, so with his burin in confident fingers he put his initials at the base of the plate. All the inks and paper he needed, he piled into a pack and, cursing once again the loss of his portfolio, set off down to the ice.

The day was chill, but noticeably warmer than it had been previously, and a fine drizzle of rain took the place of the daily snow. Already the roofs were dripping and patches of shining frozen cobbles appeared underfoot. Gideon walked carefully for fear of dropping his cargo and wished he'd remembered to fetch his cane from the shop, for it would have facilitated his progress on the still icy thoroughfare. He was so busy concentrating on the pavement and where to place his feet that he didn't see Mordecai until the boy bashed straight into him at a dead run.

"Whoa! Mord? What..."

"I jus' got down there, guv. I weren't late. It weren't my fault—I knew you should've let me sleep down there..." The boy was out of breath and clearly in a great deal of distress. Gideon pulled the boy into the lee of a shop doorway to avoid the rain and the crowds.

"Don't be ridiculous, you'd have frozen to death. Now, stop. Catch your breath." For a second, he wondered if it was better to take the boy back to the shop, but they were more than halfway to the river. "Now—start again."

Mord looked up, and Gideon was horrified to see the urchin's face was filthy and streaked with tears. Gideon didn't think he'd ever seen Mord cry before, not even when his father had disappeared or when the cat's kittens had all died. He was a bastion of strength and Gideon was shocked.

"The press, guv. It's the press. It's gone."

Gideon stared in disbelief. "Moved? " It was the only thing he could think of—perhaps the rivermen had decided the thaw was on its way? "Where?"

"Not moved, guv. Gone. Just..." He wiped his nose on his sleeve, then stopped and pulled out a relatively clean handkerchief. "Gone. You'd better come and see. It ain't right. I could see it, but they didn't listen to me."

With a chill in his heart and stomach enough to match any ice age, Gideon let Mordecai lead him down through the streets to the river. Nothing much seemed changed; most of the stalls had finished setting up and were waiting for another day of frolic, possibly the last if the rain continued. It wasn't until they reached the ice that Gideon could see that the ice was lessening—the peaks were flattening to humps, the straw and cinders put down for safe-footing was often floating in puddles of dirty rancid water. There were ominous noises coming from the ice and Gideon didn't like being on it at all. As he approached where his stall was, he could see a crowd gathered in front, obscuring his view.

Mord dashed ahead. "Now clear out, you. Mr. Frost's here now."

The small congregation parted to let Gideon through and Gideon saw the devastation. The press had, as Mordecai had said, simply gone. A dark gaping hole, proving how thick the ice was, was all that was left of the area where only yesterday the two of them had worked side by side.

His neighbour, the apothecary, offered his condolences, but Gideon hardly heard him, simply nodded and took a step closer—as if he could possibly see his greatest possession and the means to his survival sitting there, just under the ice— waiting to be saved. But there was nothing. Just dark brown murky water racing by with uncaring speed. He closed his eyes and nearly toppled forward as the full realisation seeped its way into his mind. Gone. Everything gone. Ruined.

"'Ere, guv! Get him a chair, can't you?" He was pulled backwards and lowered into a chair. Someone gave him a hipflask and he took a drink without thinking, coughing as the foul gin hit the back of his throat. "He's had a shock. We both have. Just...leave us in peace, eh?"

A peculiar calm filled him, as if it was all happening to someone else and for a moment he thought he must be still warm in bed, surely this was just a continuation of his nightmare. Any moment now Thouless would come chasing through the crowds, scattering parchment in front of him. But as he recovered and the spirits warmed him through, the truth made itself clear to him.

"You all right now?" Mord peered anxiously at him. "P'raps you shouldn't have come down. But I wanted you to see this." He walked around the edge of the hole.

"Careful, for God's sake," Gideon said, starting up.

"It's all right. It's bloody thick 'ere. Look." He poked the edge of the ice with a stick, measuring the thickness and showing Gideon. "See? And look here. It's like...pie-crust or something, all around the edge of the hole. Little nibbles. But regular-like. All the way round."

Gideon looked. It was true; it was odd that the press would have dropped into a neat hole almost exactly the same size as it was without cracking any of the surrounding ice. The nibble marks went all the way through the ice and all the way around.

"And look here," Mord said. "There's a lot of ice been chipped off, left in heaps. It wouldn't have done that if it had just broke. And what do you think this is?" He handed Gideon the piece of broken wood he was holding. It was a piece of oak, with joints at both ends.

"It's part of the frame..." he said. The oaken frame that held the plate.

"Right," Mord said, nodding grimly. "They smashed it to bits before they cut the hole out, that's what I reckon. In case you could pull it out, in case it didn't drop down. They couldn't know how deep it was here. They didn't want to take no chances."

"They..." Gideon said it automatically, but it was hardly a question. He knew who had done this.

Mord's voice was angry, bitter and full of tears. "Well, it's got to be one of them, ain't it?" He waved over to where the other presses were. "Jealous—only they'd no need. We was small! We wasn't hurting them!"

"They didn't...No, Mord. They didn't." He stood up, feeling like he'd aged a hundred years. "Gather up what you can, if there's anything left."

"Not much. But what do you mean?"

"Just pack up what you can. And we'll talk about this back at the shop. Come on. It's over."

It's all over, he thought. Only one more thing to do, and he could put the whole life behind him for good and all.

He left Mord in the shop, sorting through what stock they had. He intended to take any printed material back down to the ice, back to the area with the terrible hole, and try and sell what he could before...before he left. There was only one choice for a man with no hope. *Well, that's not strictly true,* he thought, bitterly. *I could make my part-time activity a career.* But he'd seen men who'd been "on the town" for any length of time, and he didn't want to be one of the dead-eyed world-weary men that he saw in Lad Lane or the Churchyard. Neither did he want to find a man to "look after him." Not that he knew where one was to be found. Not on the streets, he was sure of that. Add in the fact that he was lucky enough on his occasional jaunts to the hunting grounds, but he was too old to start making a life of it. He didn't want to spend his nights with a succession of strangers and he knew that eventually he'd have to sell his arse and the thought of that—with strangers—made him feel ill.

So there was only one choice, and that was the army. The one place that he was sure would take him on. With the French in retreat, and the coldest winter for years, men were always wanted.

Gideon knew at least he'd be clothed and fed. He was desperate enough to be tempted.

Arriving finally at Joshua's house, Gideon paused at the front door, and walked around the back, suddenly conscious of his loss of status. He was no longer an artisan. With one deft stroke, Thouless had made him no better than a beggar.

The hate for the man was coiled deep inside him, and, more than that, fury at his own stupidity that he hadn't seen in time what the man was at—when it should have been obvious. Even Mord could have seen it.

A man—presumably Joshua's footman—opened the back door and looked down his nose, "Yes? What do you want?" He looked suspiciously at the tatty bag that Gideon clutched under his arm. "If you're selling anything, we aren't buying."

With an inner sigh, he straightened up and glared hard at the servant. Handed over his card and asked to see Redfern.

"Wait here," the man said, glancing at the card with a suspicious frown, leaving Gideon to try and keep warm in the cold drizzle. It was at least ten minutes until he returned and led him through the warm, stone-flagged kitchen, out of the baize door and up the stairs. He'd been so long that Gideon half suspected he had been sitting with his feet up in the kitchen, for it didn't take that long to walk through the house.

"Mr. Frost, sir," the man announced, leaving Gideon inside the door. Joshua was already on his feet and had a smile on his face a mile wide that made Gideon sick with happiness. What a joy it would be to step inside those arms, to let them enfold him, to sink his head onto Joshua's shoulder and just forget. Forget it all and let Joshua deal with everything. But that was impossible. It had always been so, and it was ten times more impossible now.

"Gideon!" The warmth in his voice was clear, as was the strength and duration of his handshake. Gideon felt tears heat his eyes at the man's friendliness. But he forced them away. "What a pleasant surprise!" Joshua looked at the bag that Gideon held and raised an eyebrow. "Don't tell me you finished ahead of time? And you were going to make me wait until tomorrow. Peters, some wine for Mr. Frost, I'm sure he needs warming."

Again, Gideon felt a leap of happiness at the obvious double entendre in Joshua's voice. It was clear that the man had taken their relationship to a new level, and as far as Joshua was concerned, it seemed, they were as good as equals. What irony that wasn't so. What terrible irony that it couldn't be less so. Gideon took the wine and waited quietly for Peters to leave, then after a large draught for courage he said what he had come to say.

"I'm sorry, sir..."

"What's this?" Joshua mocked gently. "Surely we aren't back there again?"

"Please, just listen to me." Another burst of affection from Joshua—proving that Thouless' words were right—and Gideon didn't know how long he could remain being formal. "Please."

"Gideon?" Joshua moved closer, his eyes scour-

ing Gideon's face. "You are whiter than the ghost
you normally resemble, if that's possible. What's
happened?"

Reaching into the sack he carried, he pulled
the copper plate out and placed it on the table beside them. "I can't finish it. Oh, the work is
done—it needs nothing more—but I won't now be
able to tint and print it for you. I am more sorry
than I can say."

"What happened?" Joshua, serious now, re-
filled their glasses from the decanter. "Sit down,
man, for God's sake, before you fall down."

Slowly, and carefully, Gideon related the
events of the morning. He omitted all reference to
Thouless and his commission, the visit, the attack
and the extortion. He had no proof and he could
hardly expect Joshua to believe his suppositions,
however sure he was himself. He was ashamed at
how Joshua might react to the news that Gideon
had accepted the invitation to dine; he wouldn't
understand the weakness, the temptation of a
fantastic meal, and the excuse he'd used to himself that he felt sorry for Thouless. He would see
Gideon for the weak grasping fool he now considered himself to be.

All the while, Joshua sat opposite him, his eyes
active, as if taking in every worn thread, every
line of worry, every dark shadow. From the solicitous look and anxious timbre to his voice, Gideon
began to wonder if Thouless might not be telling
the truth, but it was more likely that Redfern was
such a decent person that he'd behave the same if
any beggar turned up on his doorstep.

"What will you do?" Redfern asked finally. "Surely you can paint—draw? You have talent, Gideon."

"I'm afraid that my skills in that respect fall short. I was taught by my father and while I can dash off sketches to suit—silhouettes and some very poor caricatures—they can't compare with the artists. I know, sir," he said, interrupting Joshua as he gallantly attempted to reassure. "I've been in the trade a long time and I know what's popular. Political figures. War. Boney. Not houses, and that's what I'm best at. The best I could do is sell my wares on the street." He blushed and lowered his eyes when he realised how true that was.

"Then it's settled," Joshua said. "You'll come here."

Gideon glanced up. Joshua wasn't smiling. He looked deadly serious, and Gideon, although he didn't doubt his own ears, hardly dared to open his mouth for saying the wrong thing, because there wasn't a right thing to say. Instead Joshua continued. "It seems the perfect—the only solution."

To Gideon it didn't, but the sensible part of his mind was telling him how it could be. But under what circumstances? Eventually he found his tongue. "It's kind. Very kind of you. But I've never...I'm not...I've never been in service, sir. I don't know if I know—I've always been independent."

Redfern swept over that with all the delicacy of a French battalion. "Nonsense. Not kind at all.

Seems obvious to me. You say you can't afford to
keep the shop, and with it goes your accommodation. I've got accommodation here and to spare,
and how difficult can it be? If Peters can manage
it, the big oaf, then I'm sure an intelligent person
can pick it up. Need a valet, anyway. Need a Boots
too, if that lad of yours is in the same straits."

Gideon was floundering. Too much had happened in too short a time and his acuity was mud-
dled; he felt confused and vulnerable. He was being put on the spot and a large portion of his soul
wanted to grab this opportunity with both hands.
So what if it was service? It was *warm*, it was dry.
He'd never be hungry again and most of all he'd
be close—so close to Joshua, every day. He was a
little vague about the full role of a valet, but he
knew it must involve close attendance. Dressing—
and undressing—his master. That was nearly
enough reason to say yes—*oh God yes*—on the
spot.

Joshua was staring at him, obviously expecting
an answer and Gideon couldn't give him one. It
was too much.

Redfern misinterpreted his reticence. "Of
course I interrupted you... If you do have a better
offer?"

Gideon surveyed his options; there was the
army. It had seemed such a viable—if unpleasant—option such a short while ago. But it was the
middle of a freezing cold winter and the thought of
sleeping in barracks, and marching in dead men's
boots seemed unpalatable against the lure of living in this gracious house, even if it was in the

servant's quarters. He was quite sure Joshua's servant's quarters were far better than his own home. But was that reason enough?

Then there was Duncan. Time and time again, Duncan had offered him a partnership, with generous terms. Nothing up front and a reduced portion of the profits until he'd paid his stake in the business. In return, he'd have to billet in with Duncan (the boys slept in a separate room at least). He wouldn't be sweeping chimneys but canvassing, doing paperwork and supervising sweeping gangs, thereby doubling the size of Duncan's operation. And in addition, he'd still be independent, which had always been so important.

But then...he thought, hopelessly. Why would he be more independent there than he would here? And if he took Duncan up on the offer, would Duncan want more than Gideon was willing to give? Was that the only reason he wanted him to come in with him?

He looked up, aware that Joshua was waiting for some answer, and the man's face caught him unawares. In one second he saw that Thouless was right. Joshua's look of fragile hope gave him everything he wanted to know and he threw caution to the winds. So what if he was lowering himself? So what if he was losing his own life, and taking on the borrowed glory of someone else's? Joshua cared enough to look so worried that he might so say no. So how could he? The gulf between them would widen impossibly, but seeing Joshua daily would make up for that.

He smiled, suddenly feeling tired, as if someone had taken a huge weight from his back and was telling him that now—at last—he could rest. "Yes," he said softly, almost as an experiment, to see what Joshua did, and he almost laughed at the sheer joy on the other man's face. "I think you're right. It would be the best option—for me, at least. I'll have to ask Mordecai. And I will, when I go for my things."

"Dash it, there's no need for that," Joshua interrupted. "I can send a man around for that. Bring the boy back too, if you like."

"No." Gideon stood, wearily. "I would rather finish matters up in that life. Things that need to be done."

"Then come back tomorrow," Joshua said, and Gideon felt stupidly grateful at the warmth and welcome in the man's words. *He's your master now, Gideon. He can't be your friend.* Leaving the bag with the copper plate under his chair, he stood and took his leave. As he shook hands with Joshua he realised that this was the last time they would meet in these almost equal circumstances. He treasured the feel of the man's hand in his all the way to the Strand.

Elated, Joshua reached for the bell-rope after Gideon had been seen to the door. He gave orders to Peters to prepare a room for Gideon and had to school his features carefully not to show his elation. He had been shocked at Gideon's story, and he felt most badly for the young man—he could not imagine what it must be like to lose everything that you'd been working so hard to maintain all of your life—but he could not help but wonder if it was, as his father had always said, fated to be. He loved Gideon, lusted for his touch, his presence, the sight of him, and here he was, delivered on to him, almost in response to some unuttered prayer.

He was sure that he could help Gideon. As much as he longed to keep the man by his side forever, he couldn't see him satisfied with the post of a valet forever. Schemes and ideas swirled around in Joshua's head, each one more implausible than the last, each daydream sweeter than the one before. He imagined himself as Gideon's mentor, his patron, setting him—one day—back in business with a new press and a new shop with "Sponsor: Joshua Redfern" across the door. And then one day, Gideon might turn to him in gratitude, slide his hand into his own and press those sweet lips to his face.

Redfern felt himself hardening at the very thought of it, the way he always did whenever any daydreams of physical contact with Gideon plagued him. He wondered how it would feel to have him naked and pliant, held tight against him. How his skin would feel, as his fingers traced the line of his backbone from that elegant neck, along the delicious curve of his back to the heaven—and entirely imaginary perfection of his arse. His cock began to ache as he closed his eyes for a second and flexed his fingers, visualising how that arse would feel as his hands closed over it. Lean, he was sure. Very little fat, and hard, harder when Gideon clenched. And what else, what delights awaited him? He shook his head and opened his eyes, letting the vision and phantom body in his arms work its magic, letting the lust course down, down into his loins.

God. He was in danger of spending his seed here in his drawing room without even touching himself. If Gideon's imaginary form could have this effect, what might his real body do? Whatever it might do, Joshua was quite sure it would not be a disappointment. He strode to the door and took the stairs two at a time, flinging open his bedroom door and slamming it behind him, grateful that he was currently without a valet. In the seclusion of his room, he allowed himself to revisit his vision of Gideon, grateful, sweet and entirely naked in his arms. Releasing his cock from his breeches, he grasped it firmly, then groaned as the imaginary Gideon dropped to his knees and engulfed the end of Redfern's swollen cock in that beautiful, wide mouth. *Oh God*, he thought. *Would he look at me like I'm imagining he would as he swallows me? Would he welcome me as I move back and forwards in his mouth—like this?* He pumped gently into his hand, his eyes tight closed as his vision lapped and sucked at him.

It was too much, too much. With one fist pressed hard against his mouth, he came, and his seed pulsed over his sliding fingers. It was needful, cathartic, but it wasn't satisfying, and never would be until his dreams came true.

As he washed, his thoughts drifted to Lt. Neil Pearson and how his indiscretion had led to his death. It still hurt him; not just the brutal death

that his lover suffered, but that it was the court-
martial and hanging that had brought the facts
that Neil had a lover on board ship to Redfern's
attention, and Redfern had been unable to do anything but stand by and let his lover die, without
being able to show one glimmer of emotion. Since
then Redfern had not sought out intimate companionship, finding relief only in the bodies of the
rent boys and not often doing that, either. The
thought of anything happening to Gideon turned
his stomach; he knew he wouldn't be able to take
another loss.

He swore to himself that he'd never bring any
danger to Gideon, that once he was under his roof
he'd care for him. Protect him. Even if it meant
that the only time they'd couple would be in Redfern's vivid but frustrated imagination.

CHAPTER EIGHT

"So, what do you want to do?"

"It ain't fair, guv, and that's the bleeding truth of it." Mordecai's face was grimy with tears, and set in anger.

"No. It's not. But we have no proof. You can't just go throwing accusations out about people like that. You are lucky that Green decided not to have you charged for slander. Look, Redfern's a decent man..."

"I ain't going into service, and that's the start and end of it, guv. And you shouldn't, neither. You're better'n that. I seed what it did to our Gabriel..." He stopped, and bit his lip.

"It's all right. I'm sorry, Mord. I forgot." Gabriel had been a year older than Mordecai, sent as hall boy at Lord Wensum's country house. From the little they'd patched together after the boy had died, it seemed he worked sixteen hours a day, seven days a week, on nothing much more than porridge. And no one found that surprising.

"I promised then I wouldn't."

"I understand, truly, although Mr. Redfern is a decent man."

"But is his footman decent? Is his butler decent? It don't make no never mind if he is if they ain't. I won't. I'm sorry, guv. I'd do mostly anything to stick with you, but I won't do that."

"So..."

"Don't worry about me. There's always work if you want to work hard enough." He sighed. "What about Muffin?"

Gideon laughed then, a short laugh that surprised them both. "Mord, you are a strange boy. Here we are facing ruin, and you worry about that flea-merchant. You can take her with you. Whether she stays is up to her, as usual."

They were silent for a while, packing up into two boxes, things they could sell on the ice, and things they should be able to hawk around the other printers—tools, inks, acids. Then Mord said, "You like that Mr. Redfern, don't you?"

Gideon's stomach gave a flip; he'd tried so hard to keep his preferences from the boy. "He's a good man. I can save a little, and in a few years, perhaps..."

Mordecai stopped packing for a second, his hands gripping the edges of the crate, his knuckles white. "We ain't never going to have enough money to set up again, guv, and you don't have to coat it with honey for me. I gets it. I'll be all right." He turned away and started shoving inks into the crate. "Right. I'll get round the Street with this lot. I won't come back 'til I've sold 'em all, and I won't let no one rook me neither."

"I know you won't, Mord. We'll need every penny to pay off Simeon." Without another word, the boy was gone out into the street, leaving Gideon to finish up, his thoughts like tangled silk, too complicated to think through.

"But that's simply frightful, Joshua," Thouless was all solicitation. "Has he reported it to the Runners?"

"He says it's pointless. Have to agree with him there."

"But not to report it at all? Seems rather ingenuous, what? Surely it would be better so to do? If of course it *was* deliberate destruction in the first place."

"What the devil do you mean by that?" Joshua asked. "Of course it was deliberate. How else would it have happened?"

"Oh," Thouless waved an airy hand, his cuffs waving with just the effect he planned to create. "How would I know? I didn't see the damage. Neither did you. But this man who you've met perhaps three times in your life comes to you with this—tale—and you don't doubt one word of it. You are a decent person, Joshua. You tend to believe what people tell you."

Redfern glowered. "I believe Gideon." It wasn't until Thouless' eyebrow raised that he realised his faux-pas.

"My dear," Thouless said. "I'm not saying that the young man is lying. God forbid that I would throw suspicion on his motives in running to you. I'm just expressing surprise at him not going to the authorities. As you or I would if our property had been stolen or damaged." He examined his nails thoughtfully. "It's rather obvious that his business has been in a bad way for some time, though, isn't it?"

"What's that got to do with anything?"

"Oh, nothing, nothing... But wasn't it you that was telling me that story of your cousin's friend of a friend who was sent to the Fleet and had his own warehouse burned to the ground? I must say, Joshua, you do know the shadiest of people."

"I don't *know* Swainson! I don't think even Harry does. It was just a story I heard, damn you. And I don't know if it holds any more water than Frost's story. But I can't help but believe him, Finn."

"Well, of course not."

Redfern gave a grunt. "You were not here. He was... he seemed broken."

"He *seemed*? Hmm. Well, I'm pleased that he had someone to turn to."

"What's the devil's the matter with you, Finn? I thought you liked him well enough?"

"Oh, he's attractive enough in an obvious way, I suppose. Did I tell you young Eltham said that he thought he knew him? From...somewhere?"

"Eltham?" Redfern felt a shockwave flood through him. "That...molly?"

The look on Thouless' face was a study, and for the first time Redfern wondered if Thouless was as entirely ignorant of his own preferences as he pretended to be. "I'd hardly call him a molly," he said. "Just a little eager for all kinds of experiences, perhaps. He does have two children."

"And he's never at home and dresses like a bloody castrato," Redfern said with feeling. It was men like him that put other men with the same proclivities in such danger. Men who seemed to want to announce it to the world that they were unnatural—and the world perceived them as a real threat. "Where did he say that he knew Frost from? He'd been to the shop?"

Thouless laughed, an unpleasant little sound. "Oh, no. I don't think so. He doesn't have money to waste on art. I think he said he met him somewhere quite unlikely."

"If you've got something to say, Finn, then spit it out." He felt uncomfortable; all the seemingly harmless gossip and vitriol his friend had ever shared about others seemed suddenly dangerous and personal. How many times had he listened to Finn gossip about others, Eltham and the rest?

"All right," Thouless sighed. "He said it was at St Paul's Churchyard or Lad Lane—somewhere of that nature. If you really must know. Are you satisfied now?" He took a step back, as if to better survey the effect the words had on Redfern.

"I don't believe it for one moment."

"I admit to being a little shocked meself. I would never have imagined it, would you? He doesn't look the type—but you did say his fortunes did tend to be a little...hit or miss, didn't you? Of course, I wouldn't have mentioned it at all if you weren't considering taking him into your household. You'll think twice now, I'll wager."

It was all Redfern could do to stay immobile, to stop himself from lashing out, or calling out his friend. Thouless' words had hit him like a sledge-hammer. He couldn't believe it, wouldn't believe it. It was just that Eltham was mistaken, that's all it was. That's what it had to be.

As he sat there staring into the fire something dawned on him, and he looked up at Thouless to see a look of sardonic amusement on his friend's face. *He does know,* he thought, and somehow that didn't seem a relief, the way he'd thought it would be. Suddenly it didn't seem safe. *And it means that Gideon—likes men.* His heart sank, and the treacherous thought came battering at him. *Or at least sells himself to them.*

"Anyway," Thouless said lightly, "it's only Eltham's word, isn't it? I'd be more worried about your deposit if I were you. If it *was* your pretty new valet, then I'd watch your purse. Eltham said he gave him a guinea for services in advance and the rogue ran off into the fog. What about your deposit? I'll warrant that Frost never returned it."

"I would imagine he's attempting to salvage what's left. He's no crook, Finn, whatever else he might be guilty of." He pointed to where the canvas bag was still sitting under the chair on the other side of the room. "He brought me the plate of the engraving. He could have—should have—asked me for the price of it, or at least the materials he'd used, but he didn't."

"But the deposit would have more than covered that, wouldn't it?" Thouless scooped up the bag and pulled the plate from inside. Something inside Redfern churned with jealousy. He didn't want Thouless' hands on the plate for some reason. "It's good enough work, I'll say that for him, even if he didn't finish it in time."

Redfern took the plate from Thouless. He couldn't disagree. He couldn't imagine what the finished article would have been like, what colours and tints would be visible, but the quality of the etching was remarkable; every leaf, every brick almost completely represented.

"Well, I'll leave you to it, Joshua my dear," Thouless picked his hat up from a chair. "I think you are making a mistake trying to tame that young man, but I hope that I'm wrong." He paused and put a hand on Redfern's shoulder and Redfern had to restrain himself from brushing the hand away. It was startling how quickly he felt antipathy towards the man. Had he really considered him his best friend? "Just be careful, and I'll see you next Sunday." At Redfern's blank look, he continued. "Your brother's birthday?"

Redfern grimaced. He'd forgotten all about it. No getting out of it, but now it seemed deuced awkward and frankly perilous under the circumstances. He waved distractedly at Thouless as he left, wondering how he could now, after their close friendship, start reducing the time he spent with the man. *Damn*, he thought. The best way out of this entire situation would be to tell Gideon that he'd changed his mind, but he knew he could never do that, no matter what tales Thouless made up about him. He knew that his affection for

Gideon went a lot further than a surface attraction.

Just let me be alone with him, he thought, his whole body tingling at the very idea. *Let me talk to him, tell him to deny the rumours. Let me look after him. That's all I want.*

Even as he finished the thought he knew it wasn't true. He wanted more, a lot more, and now perhaps there might be a hope that he'd get it.

CHAPTER NINE

The little furniture he'd owned was in a cart outside, and a merchant was strapping it down. All the stock they could sell had been sold. The printing community had been generous, wiping away any doubts that Mord had had about their involvement in the press's destruction. Gideon was sweeping the floor when the bell sounded and Duncan appeared shaking the rain off his coat.

"What the blazes?" He took a step into the shop and grasped Gideon by the upper arms. "It's true then. I thought they were playing some kind of sick joke on me." He looked around the shop, which didn't take long. "And when were you planning on telling me?"

"It all happened a bit quickly." Gideon shook his friend's hands off. "There's nothing anyone can do."

"And it's true you are going into service too, is it?"

"Stop shouting at me, for God's sake. Yes. It's true."

"Are you mad?"

"No. Take a look around, will you? See anything missing? What do you suggest? That I place myself on Lad Lane forever? Become some powdered darling to a poxed old madge-cull? Because it's not that appealing to me. At least a valet is a decent trade."

"And what do you know about it? Gideon, turn around and look at me, will you? Come in with me—it's perfect, you know I want..."

"It's not what I want. I'm sorry—I am. What do I know about sweeping?"

"I'll show you, it's..."

"No." There was steel in Gideon's voice. "Don't you understand? I'm tired, Duncan. I'm tired of being cold and hungry and sleeping on more lumps than bed. I'm tired of sitting up all night designing so that I can work the press all day. I'm tired of fighting every day, tired of dodging debts and tired of walking up that hill to St Paul's and hating myself more and more every time I do it. I'm tired of hoping that 'tomorrow will be the day I start to make a profit' and... Damn. I'm just tired."

Duncan said nothing for a long time and then sighed. He put a hand on Gideon's shoulder, and when he spoke, his voice was soft. "I understand, Gid. It's just that you've always been a fighter."

"Yes. Well. I had weapons. I had hope. Now I've got nothing but the offer of a job, and I'm going to take it."

"Is this the pretty Irishman?"

"No. It's not." The violence in Gideon's voice was obvious and Mord, cleaning windows in the back, looked around curiously. "It's a Mr. Redfern, Charles Street." He didn't want to volunteer anything further.

"I can't help but be suspicious, Gid. Why is he taking you on? You've got no experience."

"He's a client."

"From the Churchyard?" Duncan's whisper was thoroughly shocked.

"No, of course not. From here."

"Well, I don't like it. I bet the first opportunity he gets he'll have his hands in your smallclothes. No one takes on a valet because they have altruistic leanings."

"You're wrong, Duncan. He's all right."

"Well, it's your funeral. Your first day off, you'll meet me?"

"I don't know. I can't say. Look, Duncan, I'll let you know, all right? I'll send you a note."

"Through the boy? Is he coming with you?"

"No, he's not. Mordecai."

Duncan turned to Mord. "Mordecai? If you need a job, you know where I live."

Mordecai stopped cleaning but he didn't turn around. "Thanks, Mr. Verney. I'll think about it."

Gideon took Duncan's hand and squeezed it warmly. "Thank you," he mouthed, silently. And he didn't shy away when Duncan stole the swiftest of kisses.

"If you need me," Duncan said as he pulled the door open, "and I don't mean... Damn, you *know* what I mean, Gid." Gideon nodded. "If you need anything I can give, or do. You shout, and you shout loud." Then he was gone.

Saying goodbye to Mord was one of the hardest things he'd ever done and they were both fighting tears by the end of it. Mord had almost promised that he'd take Duncan up on his offer and Gideon promised to stay in touch.

Finally alone in the little shop, Gideon allowed himself a moment of grief, then taking his hat and cane, and ramming his hat onto his head with a determined air, he said, " I'm sorry, Father," and stepped out to find his new life.

He hadn't really known what to expect below stairs at Joshua's house, hadn't allowed himself to think about it, if truth be told, but he was surprised at the welcome he received. There was a certain amount of curiosity from all, questions upon questions that he answered, or fielded as best he could, until Peters—Mr. Peters, he was now to Gideon, stopped them with a swift air of command. There was no doubt who was second in command in this household. Mr. Peters ran the house well and Gideon spent his first full day with the staff, not even venturing into the main house at all. He learned the names, and the routine. He found that he was Mr. Frost to all of the staff, but that Mr. Peters and Mrs. Denton could call him Gideon at table. He could call the lower staff by their given names but never the cook or butler. He was measured for clothes, fed until he thought he would burst and shown his room, reached by a circuitous route from the servants' quarters by a system of bare passageways and staircases.

His meagre possessions sat on a bed which looked better than most things Gideon had slept on. On the wall above the bed there were two bells. Mr. Peters continued his instruction: "The smaller bell is connected to the servants' hall and the larger is from Mr. Redfern's suite. You have your own bell downstairs, as you know, but this ensures that you are available for Mr. Redfern at all hours."

Gideon blushed at that, and was grateful for the dim light in the tiny room. It was, he was pleased to see, a single room and he remarked upon that.

"It is because you are now, Mr. Redfern's confidential servant, as am I."

Gideon nodded.

"I understand you've not done this work before?"

"I'm ashamed to say I have not. I am surprised that Mr. Redfern gave me the opportunity."

Peters' impressive implacability gave nothing away and Gideon wondered exactly what the man knew. "The daily duties are not onerous. The fires are laid by the staff, of course, and the bulk of the washing and pressing too. You'll be responsible for ensuring that his clothes are in good condition, clean and ready to wear. You'll have to learn what he wears where and anticipate his needs. I have been doing this in the absence of a valet and can help you with anything you require. But," and the butler's voice softened a little, "he's the best employer I've had. He doesn't fuss if his house runs smoothly. And that's my concern. The more technical matters such as Mr. Redfern's accounts, bills, travel arrangements we can deal with as they come up."

"It's kind of you, Mr. Peters."

"Not at all. I'll be pleased to be rid of the work. Now. Shaving. Most important and the first task you'll need to be prepared for in the morning. Have you ever shaved another man?"

"I have, yes. My father, after he lost the use of his arm."

"Excellent. Now it just remains to show you the private route from here to Mr. Redfern's suite and I'll let you get unpacked. Servants' dinner is at eight, after Mr. Redfern has eaten, earlier if he's dining out. In the morning you'll come down to the hall, take shaving water to his rooms, then return for his breakfast. He rises at nine most mornings, but you'll need to be up at six." The butler smiled. "Don't look so stricken, Gideon, yours is a good position—and you get to eat before your day's work begins, which is more than most of the staff here can say."

He led Gideon through a second door from his room, explaining, "Only you have access to his room through this corridor, the rest of us go through the house, even me. The lamps are always kept lit." He opened a large oak door at the end and led him through.

Joshua's bedroom was larger than any bedroom Gideon had ever seen in his life, panelled from ceiling to floor in dark wood. A large wardrobe stood on one side, flanked by a pair of magnificent chests of drawers. The bed dominated the room; not a curtained monstrosity like his father's had been, but a wide, elegant construction; a decorative carved headboard standing guard at the top of an expanse of expensive snowy linen. Gideon felt decidedly grimy, glad he didn't have to touch the pristine whiteness.

"The maid will bring you linen," Peters continued, "but you will be responsible for the bed itself."

"Where is Mr. Redfern now?" He felt nervous being in these rooms and wondered how he'd cope when there was just him and his master alone.

"He went into town earlier today, and said he would not be back until late, not requiring any dinner." The man pulled open drawer after drawer, showing Gideon where everything was, cravats, stockings, shirts. The quality of everything took Gideon's breath away. "You'll need to be on hand when he returns, however late, to draw a bath if he needs it."

Gideon followed Peters into a long tiled bathroom, with mirrors down each side. There was a peculiar tub at the far end with a tent-like canopy over it and Peters saw Gideon staring at it. "Don't worry," he said, "it's very simple." He took a small ladder from beside the tub and mounted it. You simply pour hot water into the funnel at the top and it pours in a shower of rain over the master."

Gideon found he was staring at the device, imagining the long, lean length of Joshua standing below while he poured warm water over his naked body.

I don't know if I can do this, he thought, *not without having my body betray me at every step.*

"It's quite simple," Peters said, misinterpreting Gideon's stricken expression. "And the master doesn't often require it. He prefers a bath, although that's a lot more work."

When Peters left him, Gideon unpacked and sat staring into space for what seemed like hours. Had he made the biggest mistake of his life? Was he stupid? Stubborn and stupid not to take Duncan up on an offer that was no worse than this? He lay back on the bed, and was unable to discount the comfort of the mattress into his calculations, as he slowly drifted into sleep.

He was woken in the dark by a harsh ringing which made him leap up. Confused he glared into the darkness and reached down beside the bed for his flint and candle. Not there! It was then that he remembered where he was.

The ringing continued; he cursed himself for not making sure he knew the sound of each bell before falling asleep, and tried to remember where the door was. Carefully he made his way to the wall, found a handle and turned it. Muted gaslight flooded into the room, showing him it was the kitchen bell, which was a huge relief, for if it had been Joshua, he'd hardly have made a good impression.

Splashing cold water on his face and hands, he made his way back down the service route to the kitchen, congratulating himself when he only missed his way once.

"Mr. Frost, come in and sit down. Move there, Betsey, and let Mr. Frost sit in Mr. Gooding's old place." The cook beckoned him in and gratefully he sank into the seat allocated to him. "Master's not back yet, but we didn't think he would be. Dare say he's out with Mr. Thouless and Mr. Cooperstone. He's not a great one for parties, is Mr. Redfern, but he does like his cards."

"Now then," Peters admonished, "we don't want Mr. Frost to think that we gossip." Mrs. Denton waited until Peters turned to collect the carving tools and gave Gideon a huge wink.

"Of course not, Mr. Peters."

Grace was said and the meal partaken, mainly in silence. Mr. Peters made polite conversation with Mrs. Denton, but other than that, it was a time when the butler reminded the staff of jobs yet to do before retiring. "I would wait down here, Mr. Frost," he advised Gideon. "I'll receive the master, and will advise you of his needs. You will then have time to enter his rooms before he's finished his brandy. Betsey will put water on to heat and it will be taken up for you if needed."

He did as he was told, feeling out of place and the only person without a task. The house ran smoothly enough, he noticed. Various maids scuttled around with buckets and mops, others helped Cook clean up, light lights, floors were scrubbed. Mrs. Denton seemed the only one willing to talk—hardly surprising as everyone else was so busy—and her good-natured gossip kept Gideon from falling asleep again, warm and weary in front of the fire.

The butler appeared at last. "He's here, Mr. Frost, and he's in the drawing room. I've told him you are here, and there's hot water been sent up. You get up to his room now, lay out his night things. Take the hot-bottle with you. Quickly."

Gideon fled, feeling the power of Peters' command for the first time. In no time at all, he was inside Joshua's suite and wondering how his life had changed so very quickly. Yesterday morning he had no one to please but himself, perhaps Mord. Now he had to please two men at the very least. He pulled down the sheets, placed the pottery bottle in the middle of the bed, then hunted around for a nightshirt and slippers. It seemed to take forever, but he finally located them in the last drawer he searched. The shirt went into the bed and the slippers in front of the roaring fire.

Then he just stood around, feeling a little useless, and bone-tired, wanting to sit down but knowing that it wouldn't be acceptable. Eventually, he heard Joshua's voice outside the door and his heart leapt "No, go to bed, Peters," and the door opened.

CHAPTER TEN

h God, Joshua thought, *he's here.* Gideon Frost, in his bedroom, at last. It wasn't exactly how he hoped it would happen, but it had happened. Gideon was standing by the bed as if completely lost, and Joshua assumed he was probably feeling that way too. He couldn't help but smile at him, but when Gideon smiled back, all Joshua could hear was Thouless' insidious voice. *"Lad Lane or one of those places."*

So what, his mind rebelled, *it's not like you haven't been there. But I was buying...doesn't that make a difference?* He shook his thoughts away as he untied and peeled off his neckcloth. Gideon hurried forward to take it. The silence was unbearable, and for the first time Joshua realised the effect of the collar he'd put around Gideon's neck.

"Has Peters shown you around?"

"Yes, sir."

Joshua took hold of Gideon's arm. "No. This changes nothing, Gideon."

"I rather think it does."

"I won't let it. Were we not trying to be friends?" There, he'd said it. "Would we not have succeeded?"

Gideon was silent for a while, but he hadn't pulled his arm away from Joshua's hold. His head was tipped down, as if he was debating something important.

"Gideon?"

"I...we...we would have been, yes. It's too late now." Gideon raised his head and looked Joshua directly in the face, and to see him looking so damned lost was all the encouragement Joshua needed. He pushed away Thouless' accusations. He didn't care. He didn't want to know and he didn't care.

"No. I won't have you say that." Though he was scarcely aware of it, his thumb was massaging Gideon's arm. "I want..." *Damn it*, he thought fiercely, *how did I manage this with Neil?* Ah yes, he remembered. Neil had kissed him in thanks for a gift. He leaned forward and kissed Gideon's cheek, wondering at his own temerity.

"Gideon?"

"Sir?" Joshua was about to reprimand him but found Gideon was smiling.

"What do you want?"

"I think it's a good start, sir." He pulled away gently. "Let's take it slowly, though, shall we?"

The next few days were some of the happiest in Gideon's life, and certainly the happiest he'd had since his father had died. He found working for Joshua to be easier than he expected and every day when he woke he had something wonderful to look forward to: seeing the man he loved. He had no doubt about it; it had moved from a hopeless passion to a deep emotion. He wanted to do his best for Joshua, and he worked hard to do so. Somehow he didn't find the work menial—in fact, there was little manual labour to be done, for the room was cleaned by other staff, the fires built by the chambermaid, water brought up by a line of servants. But from the moment that he pulled Joshua's curtains aside every morning to the moment that Joshua kissed him gently goodnight, he enjoyed every moment they spent together.

It was more than clear to Gideon that his relationship to his master was not a typical valet-master alliance, that it resembled a gentle courtship more than paid employment, but it made every day a pleasure and never had he looked forward to work so much.

So far Joshua had only kissed him, and it was almost chaste; a peck as he got out of bed, another after his shave. Gideon secretly called them his tips and he'd often lingered after being dismissed, the way a cabbie does when he feels he's owed a little extra. When Joshua noticed this, he'd laugh, grab Gideon and kiss him with a little more passion. Gideon wondered if Joshua was afraid he'd break; the big man was a lot more gentle than he'd expected him to be. But the courtship was sweet, and the tang of danger made it even more exciting. He was in love, and he was happy.

Matthew's birthday party had been a success; Thouless and Matthew had managed to stay away from each other, and when the party finally broke up, everyone was more than a little drunk. As Gideon helped him undress that night, he attempted to take him into his arms several times only to be eluded, time and again, as Gideon escaped.

There was something that had to be addressed, though; all night Thouless had been poisonous in his assertions regarding Gideon's alleged whoring. *Just ask him, Joshua, that's all. Ask him, get a denial and I'll say no more about it. But I think you need to ask him, before this goes too far.*

With the weight of alcohol pressing down on his brain and dulling his mind, he spoke the words without thinking them through.

"Gideon, there's something I have to ask you. Something I've been meaning to ask for a while."

"Joshua?" Gideon took his jacket. "Ask away."

"I heard something. Something stupid. That I find hard to believe. About you." Gideon didn't reply but turned away and put the jacket in the wardrobe. "That you were up at St Paul's. Whoring."

As soon as the words were out of his mouth, he regretted them. He'd vowed he didn't want to know.

He could see the change in Gideon's demeanour. The shoulders straightened and he turned around slowly, all the light having gone from his face.

"Who told you this?"

"It doesn't matter. I shouldn't have said anything."

"If I may be excused, sir."

"Gideon!"

"If that's what you think of me, Mr. Redfern, then I'll leave you. You don't want a whore on your staff."

Gideon turned to go and Joshua felt a churn of desperation. He could let him go, and not embroil the pair of them in risk. He could. He *should*. Could his own reputation take the scandal? Would people remember his attending Neil's execution?

The devil take it. He strode to the door and grabbed Gideon by the arm. Gideon turned around and there it was, unguarded in his face; the need that mirrored his own. The *want*. Without another thought he gathered Gideon into the circle of his arms, feeling the man give one second's fight as he pushed himself away, then relief flooded through him as Gideon surrendered with a cry that was almost a muttered gasp of pain.

Gideon's face was turned away from him, his eyes closed.

"Gideon," Joshua said, hoarsely. "Look at me." Gideon didn't move and Joshua spoke again, with more authority. "Damn you, Gideon. Look at me!"

Gideon's head snapped around and his expression of want was replaced with a single command. *Kiss me.*

Joshua obeyed the unspoken command before

either of them could think for another second. There was that subtle, sublime moment again as Gideon seemed to struggle with himself, but it lasted less time than before and in a heartbeat Gideon's lips parted to give Joshua the access he'd been craving for weeks. The kiss lengthened, intensified until Gideon was pushing back at him, but this time in passion. Joshua could feel Gideon's hands at his back, at his waist, sliding down, all hesitation, all barriers between them finally, irrevocably gone.

He felt light-headed. Surely these weren't— after all this time—Gideon's arms around his neck? Were those really Gideon's muffled groans as Joshua pushed aside layer after layer of cloth, seeking skin, seeking heaven? He couldn't believe it, but when he opened his eyes and broke the kiss, there was Gideon, breathing as hard as if he'd been running, his mouth half open in pleasure and his eyes tightly closed.

"Don't stop, Joshua," he murmured, and his eyes flickered open. "Not now. Just..."

"God," was all Joshua could say. His fingers eased Gideon's shirt loose and found warm, solid flesh beneath.

They went down on the floor together, as if of one mind, forgetting the comfort of the bed, there was too much need to wait, too many clothes to be removed, too much time already wasted. Joshua pulled the clothes from Gideon—why did men wear so many damned clothes? Jacket, waistcoat—buttons ripping loose and scattering across the floor. Shirt up over the head and...there.

There. Gideon's body was wiry and slim, and Joshua's head dropped to taste the skin he'd longed for for so long. With eager, almost violent impatience, he licked and bit his way up from the waistband of Gideon's breeches, up the soft blond trail of hairs to his chest, then attacked his nipples one at a time with enthusiasm, grinning like a fool when Gideon arched off the floor as if wanting Joshua to devour every part of him.

Gideon's hands were in his hair, and his head was tipped back as he cried out softly with each fresh attack. He hooked a leg around Joshua's, and ground his hips and a sizeable erection into Joshua's hip.

Joshua needed no further invitation, pausing only to divest himself of breeches and boots before throwing himself down on top of the man, claiming his waiting kiss with his mouth and his eager hot cock with one hand. To his delight, Gideon grasped him in one swift and mutual movement and then finally, face to face, they paused and looked at each other. Joshua gave a growl as Gideon's hand moved on his prick, oh so slowly but sure, firm and so bloody good. Gideon's fingers slid down the shaft, teasing his sac with each downward movement and Joshua copied the action, watching Gideon's face as it twisted in pleasure, taking kisses whenever he could and trying to remember to breathe.

God, he wasn't going to last, that was certain. It had been too long, and he'd longed for this moment, imagined this too many times. "Gideon..." he whispered, "wait." He moved his hand over the hot flesh in his hand, pulling and squeezing, loving every sound that Gideon made.

"Too late," Gideon groaned, and Joshua kissed his words away as warm liquid flowed over his fingers. Gideon's hand tightened around his shaft, causing Joshua to spend a moment later, hot and far too fast, like a schoolboy with his first fumble.

"Gideon..." He crushed Gideon into an embrace and took kiss after kiss until they were both breathless. "Heaven."

He slid down, now that the immediate urgency had dissipated, and explored Gideon's body as he had long wanted to do. Gideon seemed perfectly at ease; languid, like a puppet with his strings cut, spread delightfully naked upon the parquet. He was smiling and his hair stood out in delightful spikes around his head.

With a grunt of impatience he clambered to his feet, pulled Gideon up, then gathered him into his arms and carried him to the warmth and comfort of the bed.

Joshua wished he had two pairs of eyes so that he wouldn't have to take his gaze off of Gideon's face, and could watch every reaction as he used his tongue on Gideon's chest and nipples. He hurried a little, sliding down in his explorations until his mouth found what it was longing for. Gideon's cock was half-hard, lying heavily against one pale thigh, and Joshua gathered it into his mouth, loving that Gideon's buttocks clenched and that he almost raised himself off the bed in pleasure.

After a few minutes of gentle sucking, Gideon was hard once more. Joshua found himself regret-

ting his age and his over-indulgence of the evening, for there was no way that he could perform
again, and he wanted to take Gideon, to claim him
for his own, to slide between that sweet cleft and
watch Gideon cry out in ecstasy. He reapplied
himself to Gideon's cock with a ready will; this he
could do, and from Neil's praise, he was sure he
could do it well.

He traced the blue vein with his tongue, and
the groan that seem to tear from the very depths
of Gideon's soul made him smile. Yes, he could do
this well. Greedily, he swallowed Gideon's length,
slipping his hands behind the man's back for lev-
erage, and kneading the rounded and muscled
cheeks, flicking his tongue back and forth rapidly
over the head and tracing the sensitive crown.
Gideon was making delightful strangled sounds,
and this spurred Joshua on. The world became
flesh; senses sharpened into intensity by the
darkness of closed eyes. He was driven on, exist-
ing only in a dark vortex of lust; every sound,
taste, touch and smell uniquely Gideon, each
of them catalogued, remembered, treasured. He
rocked over the body beneath him, devouring
every sensation as if it were his last.

It wasn't until Gideon put a hand on his head
and the world swum back into alignment that he
was even aware that Gideon had come, the taste
of semen bitter and alkaline in his throat, Gideon's cock softening in his mouth.

"Careful," Gideon said, husky and sated,
"thought you were going to drain me." Gideon held
out his arms and Joshua fell into them, and hold-

ing his love to him, he drifted into a happy sleep.

For a long time, there was nothing as he retreated behind closed eyes and let his breath slow, wallowing in the waves receding. Gideon's mind was wiped of all thought. In that blank afterglow, his senses took over. He could feel the delicious softness—*were there ever sheets so soft?*—between his fingers where he'd obviously balled them in his fist. The sharp notes of sex pervaded the air, followed by deep masculine notes of sweat and cologne. Somewhere, a bell was striking, and the sounds of the street were muffled beyond the closed curtains.

An arm was flung casually, heavily, over his ribcage, and Redfern's—no, Joshua's, it *had* to be now, of course, at least in private—*Joshua's* fingers were slowly stroking a nipple back into life. He allowed himself a huge, lung-filling breath. He felt as if he was surfacing, finally. He tipped his head slowly in Joshua's direction, and a groan of satisfaction broke from him at just that small movement.

A breath huffed in his ear, and he heard a ghost of a chuckle. "It's reassuring to an old man that he can keep up with the youth of today." Joshua's deep bass voice sent shivers down Gideon's spine.

Gideon smiled, at ease in a way he never imagined he would be. In all his fantasies about Redfern, none had encompassed this languorous after-sex feeling. He'd fantasised about the sex, many times. But he'd always ended the dream with the climax, not wanting, not daring to take it a step further and imagine this...heavenly moment of being sticky and sated in the man's all-encompassing arms. "I never thought of you as old," he murmured.

"Not too old, I hope," Joshua replied. Gideon half-expected the man to roll over and continue where he'd left off, but he didn't move, but continued to speak, in a way that sounded as if he was continuing a speech that had broken off. "We must get you sorted out, a new shop perhaps? Or maybe it might not be sensible, not right away. Maybe it would be a little obvious if I were to start visiting a printer at all hours. No, it won't do. No matter, I'll start looking around for a house that will suit us both and your assistant can move into the old shop."

Gideon went to speak at this, astounded at what Joshua was suggesting, but the larger man took that moment to roll over on top of him and silence any words with a long lingering kiss that wiped his thoughts almost entirely. It wasn't until he felt Joshua's knee pushing his own apart and Joshua's hand sliding between their bodies that he broke away, marshalling his mind, and said, "What? Move where?"

"Later," Joshua muttered, obviously intent on arousing Gideon once more. He was succeeding too, but Gideon wasn't to be distracted. With a supreme effort of will and cursing himself for stopping the attentions he'd been dreaming about for weeks, he pushed Joshua's shoulders and wrenched his face away from the kiss.

"No. Not later, *now*. What do you mean?"

Joshua propped himself up and looked into Gideon's eyes. He looked a little dazed with lust and it took all of Gideon's willpower to not be carried away by the want on his face, and to forget what he'd just heard. "I'm just saying that it won't be suitable. You staying here. I thought it would be, but I can't be bedding my valet. We need to get you set up in a nice little establishment where there won't be so much gossip."

Gideon felt himself going cold. "Gossip? *Establishment?*"

"Well, of course." Joshua smiled and Gideon felt like he was drifting backwards from the man, even though he remained propped over him. He felt he was seeing with clarity, perhaps for the first time. How could he have been so blind? Joshua was no better than Thouless, and Gideon knew he should have known. Should have listened to Duncan. Should have listened to his *head*. He wanted to turn to Joshua and to say, *I don't understand*, but he did, only too well, and Joshua's next words confirmed it.

"I've already had some comments with you being taken on the staff. It won't do. No." Joshua grazed on his neck again, his teeth nipping at Gideon's skin. His hand was cupping his balls and his treacherous cock was making a valiant attempt at a third hardening. Gideon found his control slipping and he fought to hear what Joshua was saying. "But on a quiet street, with an allowance fit to your surroundings. No one will query a young studious artist with an attentive cousin who calls in to see him several times a week."

Gideon's stomach suddenly rebelled, the port turning sour and threatening to resurface; he struggled free, wriggling out from under Joshua and rolling off and out of the covers with some difficulty, then sat on the edge of the bed, fighting with control over the bile rising in his throat.

Joshua was a heartbeat behind him, concerned and solicitous. "Gideon? You've gone white as a sheet. Here." He held out a half-full glass of wine.

Gideon pushed it away. "No." The look on Joshua's face made him feel worse. It looked as if he actually *cared*. *What a fool I am*, he thought, furious at himself. *What a copperheaded nincompoop*. He stood up, keeping his back to the bed, not wanting either to see Joshua's face or to betray his own expression of bitter, disappointed anger, and grabbed his clothes, scattered around the room. He dressed quickly. "If you'll excuse me, *sir*, I have duties."

There was a sharp intake of breath, and at that, Gideon finally turned. Joshua looked like he'd been slapped, his face tight, his teeth clenched. Slowly and deliberately, he pulled the sheet over his nakedness and drew himself up so he was sitting as proud as a king on a throne. "If you are waiting for a better offer, Frost, I'm afraid you are trying the wrong man. Perhaps one of your other clients would be more amenable."

Gideon bowed stiffly and left before another word could be spoken and fled, as quietly as he could, back up the narrow servants' stairs to his room.

He realised that that was the end of it, not
that there had been much to begin with. He'd
longed to be with Joshua, never daring to think
that it would happen. He could hardly believe that
it had all been offered to him on a silver platter. A
house, a lover, money enough to do what he liked,
and all he'd had to do was accept Redfern's generosity. Except he knew in his heart that it had
nothing to do with generosity. He'd offered him a
contract in the same way he'd asked Gideon to do
the print of the house, the same way he'd offered
him a position—and his motives had obviously
been focussed on this...arrangement all along. He
would not whore himself for this man. Not this
man, even though he'd proved himself more a man
of clay than Gideon had been imagining himself to
be.

But then, he thought treacherously, was it
really such a bad offer? Joshua hadn't exactly said
that he loved him, but Gideon was sure he did,
and, for all the danger and the proprietary as-
sumptions Joshua had made, Gideon knew that
he loved the man back. Couldn't he swallow his
pride to give them both some happiness? Wasn't
love sometimes about compromise? He battled
with his thoughts until he fell asleep, but in the
morning he was decided. If Joshua was willing to
take a risk on him, then so be it. He wondered, if
after his stiff-necked behaviour of last night
Joshua would even listen to him, but he had to
try. He loved him far too much to lose him now.

When he reached the servants' hall early next
morning, it was with a little trepidation. He knew

now just how well Peters knew this house and his master, and he was a little worried that the others would know about what occurred in the master's bedchamber after the party.

To his surprise, Gideon found no one in the hall except Peters sitting at the kitchen table, the man didn't normally come out of his pantry until breakfast. He stood as Gideon entered and Gideon felt himself go cold. *He does know.*

"The master wishes to see you immediately, Mr. Frost," the butler said.

"Now?" Gideon felt a blush rise up across his face. "I'll take his shaving water then."

"He wishes to see you in the study."

Gideon thought for a moment to ask Peters what it was about, but thought better of it. If Peters did know, he was fairly sure he wouldn't tell him, anyway. He set off at a fast walk, wondering what on earth it could be that couldn't have waited until Gideon served him breakfast. Surely Joshua wasn't so angry at his childish behaviour that he would act on it without giving him the chance to apologise?

He crossed the hall and knocked, entering when he heard Joshua's voice. The man was sitting behind his desk and Gideon felt so pleased to see him that all his misgivings left him. "Joshua, I'm sorry—" he started.

"Joshua, is it?" The voice came from behind him and Gideon spun around to find Thouless facing him. He must have been standing beside the door when it opened. "How intimate you've become in so short a time. You are as clever as I thought you were, Mr. Frost."

"What?" Gideon turned back. Joshua's face was completely impassive. "I don't understand. Can I get you anything, sir?"

"Oh, I think you understand only too well. Your little trick didn't work on me and so you go to Redfern. Not as wealthy, perhaps, but steady."

"I don't—"

"Be silent."

"No...no, I won't." Gideon looked at Joshua. "Sir? What is this about? How is it that you let him speak to me this way?"

"Be quiet, Gideon," Joshua said, and his voice, harsh and brittle, nearly broke Gideon in two. "Mr. Thouless has something to ask you."

"And I have to listen to his insinuations?"

Thouless stepped in front of Gideon and leant on the desk. "Oh, I think you'll find they are more than insinuations. Do you deny that you tried to inveigle yourself into my household in the same...position...if that's what you can call it—as you have here?"

"I certainly do! That's nonsense."

Joshua spoke, urgently as if desperate for an answer. "Did you go to his house, Gideon?"

"No—yes. Yes, I did, but it's not like that. He offered me a commission."

"Another lie," Thouless said. "What would I want of an architectural artist?"

"He wanted a silhouette," Gideon said, glaring at Thouless. "He invited me to his house."

"You may have taken my interest in your pitiful little stall on the ice as an invitation, or more likely you saw that perhaps I could offer you more than you had in reserve? You deny propositioning me?"

"I do deny it. It's a lie. You're the one who wanted something I wasn't going to give you."

"Oh, come now, you came to my house, pleading poverty and offered yourself to me, admit it."

"I utterly deny it. Joshua, you can't listen to him."

"And when I turned you down you stole from me."

"No!"

"You stole from me and ran here within a day spilling the same story of destitution you'd told me."

"No! Joshua!" Gideon stormed to the desk, almost too angry to think. "You've got to believe me, you have to. He wanted...he tried to force me..." He trailed off as he watched Joshua reach to the floor and pick up an ebony cane and place it on the desk.

"Gideon, do you deny having stolen this from Mr. Thouless?"

Gideon felt his world slipping away from him. *My cane...how could I be accused of stealing my own cane?* He tried to remember the last time he'd seen it, but he couldn't. He knew he'd brought it here, but it had just been in his room, he hadn't needed it. "Of course I deny it, it's mine."

Thouless laughed. "Oh come now, you speak of destitution and you find yourself *so badly off* that you were forced to sell yourself at the Churchyard..."

Gideon's eyes flew open wide. "You *were* the one told him..."

"Of course I told him, whore. Did you think I wouldn't? I told you I would."

"I couldn't believe you'd be so poisonous."

"I look after my friends; I don't take advantage of them."

That explains the arrangement he wanted, Gideon thought bitterly. *I should have realised.* "It's mine," he said softly.

"If you had such a valuable item, why didn't you sell it?"

"It was my father's. I don't care in the slightest what you think of me, Thouless, and I welcome your slander." He turned to Joshua. "May I speak with you alone?"

"I don't advise it, Joshua. The little thief will probably..."

"I'll speak to him. Wait outside."

Thouless went with a vicious backwards glance at Gideon. Gideon waited until the door was closed and then said, "It's mine."

"I'd like to believe you, Gideon. But I can't. What Thouless says makes sense, and you haven't been honest with me. You led me to believe that you were offended and insulted about the implications of your...money-making activities. You misled me."

"I didn't...I didn't lie to you."

"What would you call it? I've seen him with a stick exactly like this. Now the truth is that you did sell yourself at St Paul's, so how can I believe you about this?" The anger in Joshua's eyes was more than Gideon could stand.

"You think that I would steal? You think that of me? That I'm capable of that?" Gideon knew as he spoke those words that he was giving Joshua an ultimatum. He didn't know if Joshua realised it too.

"You seem to be...capable on many fronts. He won't press charges. I'll make sure of that."

Gideon laughed, a short angry bark that felt good to let out. "I wish he would. Truly I do. This way I'm guilty, and there's nothing I can say to get my good name back—and I don't care about him. But I do about you. I was stupid last night, so if this is punishment for that, I deserve punishment. I was wrong and I should have taken your offer."

"Which wasn't as good as Thouless', I assume."

Gideon stared at him, disappointment and fury flooding through him. "I'm sorry that you are so easily persuaded and that you can't listen to your heart rather than your friends. I almost told you I loved you last night. I wish I had. But if I said it now, it would be worthless to you. Perhaps it would have been worthless anyway. It's clear to me now what you think of me, over...a man like that." It hurt Gideon still more that Joshua's face didn't flicker. "Now, if you'll excuse me, sir. I have some packing to do." He left with as much dignity as he could muster, and he had to bite the inside of his cheek as he walked past Thouless, who gave him a victorious smile and salute.

He just wanted to get out. He was a fool to have thought that this would work, that the differences in their class could have ever have been breached, no matter how strong their feelings were. It was not that Thouless had poisoned Joshua's mind that hurt the most; it was that Joshua believed *him* without question. That proved to Gideon without a shadow of a doubt that that breach could have never been crossed. *Better to find out now,* he thought as he put what few things he owned into his bag. *Better...*

But he knew it wasn't, not deep down. He'd been within a whisker of begging Joshua to see reason, and that frightened him. *I let my guard down. I got too involved.*

As he let himself quietly out of the front door, not wanting to face the servants' hall, he looked up at the beautiful house he'd spent so much time etching.

No, you fool, he thought as he turned his steps towards Hyde Park. *You fell in love.*

CHAPTER ELEVEN

hree days had passed since Gideon's disgrace and dismissal, and Redfern had spent them emptying his wine cellar. Thouless, solicitous and a good friend, had been staying with him, helping him to bed when he got to drunk to stand and listening to him ramble on about his great mistake.

"Joshua, you escaped with nothing more than a flesh-wound. Imagine what would have happened if you *had* given him a house. He'd have sold the furniture in a week and left you the moment something better came along. I'll wager the man he was living with—the one who died—I'll wager it wasn't even the pup's father."

"Don't feel like a flesh-wound," he grumbled. He'd been keeping up a front with Thouless, didn't want him to see how badly he was hurt, but he missed Gideon like missing breathing. How could he have been so wrong about him? Thouless had a point, he knew nothing about Frost, he could have been any kind of trickster, seeing in Joshua nothing but a milch-cow, something to suck dry. An ambitious step up from the Churchyard.

"I feel such a fool," he said, over and over. *And guilty,* he added to himself. *Letting him go like that—if only Finn hadn't have been here, it might have been different, but then...Finn's probably right...*

"Gad, man, you'll get over it. Not the first pretty thing available. Now that I know your tastes, I'm sure I can find you a more than superior replacement. Something with an arse like marble and a cock to choke you, eh? Someone who will deserve all that you are willing to give him, and be grateful about it."

The coarseness revolted him. He didn't want anyone else. Not a replacement. Not even if he were just like Gideon. He'd have to *be* Gideon... Damn, he felt sick. Sick of closing his eyes and seeing the look in Gideon's face. Finn was grating on his nerves, and he really wanted Finn to leave, leave him alone and let him mourn his loss. But every time he insisted that he was all right, the man said that he wouldn't be any kind of friend if he left.

"You need a change of scene," Finn said. "Why don't we go to..."

Peters entered, with his usual quiet tact. "What is it, man?" Redfern asked.

Peters looked a little discomfited, and most unlike his collected self. "There is a...young...a boy to see you, sir."

Redfern turned, his head splitting. "I told you I was not at home, and particularly to boys. Give him a penny and tell him we need no jobs done."

"If you'll forgive me, sir, the young person came—quite boldly if I may say—to the front door. He was quite insistent. He says it's about Mr. Frost, sir."

Thouless stirred lazily in his chair, as if offended to be so interrupted. "Probably another complainant, Redfern. A boy sent by his master to complain of another theft of property. You can't be responsible for everything the whore did, man. Have the boy sent off. Send him to the Runners if his master has a case."

Joshua waved a hand, and if Thouless hadn't attempted to rule him in his own house, yet again, he probably would have done just what the man had suggested. All he wanted was to start forgetting Gideon. Forgetting his sweet eyes and mouth. To forget the bitter expression on Gideon's face when he'd seen him for the last time. But he would not be dictated to, so he sighed heavily and took another large glass of port. "Send the brat in, Peters."

"I don't advise..." Thouless began, but Joshua cut him off with an angry wave which knocked the glass from the table beside him, shattering it into a hundred crystal fragments.

"You've made your feelings clear," he snapped, angry at last. "Allow me to manage matters *in my own house* for once. By God, Finn—if you want to remain my friend, be silent, for I've had enough of your counsel to last me 'til Doomsday."

"You can't blame me for the whore's—"

"And I said STAY SILENT!" With a roar and a truly black expression, Redfern's temper unleashed itself. "Things would not have come to this pass if you'd kept your opinions and advice to yourself!"

He was gratified to see Thouless blanch and to concentrate on the glass in his hands, and, better still, to say nothing else, although his glance slid to the door as if expecting Gideon himself to return and say...what? Joshua hardly knew—but suddenly he was suspicious. Finn looked like a rat stuck in a trap. Redfern knew guilt when he saw it. *What's he hiding?*

Peters returned, and accompanying him was a small scruffy youth dressed in ragged black. His face and hands gave a clear indication of his trade as a sweep.

Peters pushed the boy forward. "This is the master, boy. Say your piece and go."

Joshua was confused; the boy looked somewhat familiar, but he could not place him. If he was a sweep's boy—what charge could he have against Gideon?

"Speak up," he ordered, wishing the ordeal over, wishing Thouless himself gone so he could start forgetting, and drowning himself in spirits seemed a good idea as any. "I'm told you have some accusation about a man who was employed here. Before you speak, I want you to be aware and to tell whoever sent you that I take no responsibility for the actions of any of my staff if it doesn't take place on my property." He gestured to

Peters to let go of the boy. "You can go, Peters."

Strangely, the boy waited until Peters had left the room before speaking, but when he had he unleashed a tirade at Redfern. "You! How could you? How could you believe that of the guv—I mean, Mr. Frost? What'd he do to you to blacken his name—when he was already down about as far as he could go?" Through his half-drunken haze, Redfern had to smile, for the furious, grubby boy was not what he was expecting. "You sit there, you—and HIM, who ain't fit to lick your—or Mr. Frost's—boots, as if he was your friend and he ain't! He's a liar, and a Captain Sharp, a crook and a bully!"

Shaking his head, Redfern sat up. "It would only take me to raise my voice to have you evicted—or arrested, boy, so mind your tongue when you talk of my friends."

"He ain't yer friend. He ain't! I know what Mr. Frost thought of you—no, he ain't never told me nothing, but I knew him—know him." The boy shook his head as if angry with himself. "He thought everything of you. Looked up to you, wanted to do his best work for you, his very best. He could've knocked up your piece in a day or two, but not 'im. I ain't seen him never work so hard for anyone, staying up late with his candle, wasted several plates he did, that he couldn't afford, not 'til he was happy. He wanted to please you. And you drives him off—believing that man's lies. That man—who destroyed our press, and our living!"

Redfern realised at last why the boy was familiar—Gideon's little assistant, no wonder he hadn't recognised him in his rags and soot. He turned sharply to look at Thouless; not to accuse him, for the boy's claims were ridiculous, but to see how he took to these charges.

To his amazement, the man, instead of sneering and being amused by the boy's vitriol, was pale and obviously violently angry. He stood and went to move towards the boy, hand raised as if to strike him. Redfern moved faster than he thought he was capable, putting himself between the two.

"What are you thinking of, Finn? He's just a child, no threat to you."

"Ain't I, though?" the boy went on, "Ain't I? He knows I am. Ask him, sir! Ask him what he offered Mr. Frost the day before our press got broke up."

"What does he mean, Finn?"

"He knows! Mr. Frost had a 'pointment to see him the night before. He came to the Fair and asked the guv to call on him."

"Quiet for a moment, boy. Finn? Did you?"

"And why not? I believe I told you I'd been down to the ice that day, and that your golden boy was selling himself to the masses."

The boy spat something incoherent and launched himself at Thouless, and Redfern had to hold him back. He walked the boy backwards and pushed him into a chair, trying not to think of the damage caused to the cream-coloured fabric, or the complaints he'd get from Peters. "Stay there. Move again and I'll have you thrown onto the street, Gideon or no Gideon." The warm look that the boy threw him was not lost on him and he turned back to Thouless.

"So, you were at Frost's stall, and you *did* offer him a commission?" He hardly needed to wait for Thouless' reply for the man's face gave him away. How could he have been taken in by this man? Why hadn't he seen the deceit in his eyes? He could hardly believe the boy's accusations, but *something* had Finn rattled, and he was determined to get to the bottom of it. "You said you hadn't, that Gideon was lying."

What else had Gideon been telling the truth about? Damn. Damn, *damn.* Everything that seemed so certain seemed to be slipping away from him.

"And what of it?" Thouless had attempted to regain some of his equilibrium. "He was a liar, and a whore, and a thief."

"He weren't!" the boy exploded. "He never stole nothing in his life. What...whatever else he did, he did to make a livin'."

"I'm afraid he did, boy," Redfern said. "There's no doubt of it."

"What's he supposed to have stole?"

"You don't have to explain matters to that beggar's brat, Joshua. He's obviously in league with Frost. Keeping us detained here, while Frost and his friend the sweep are probably robbing my home of further goods. Call the Runners. Throw him out."

But Redfern was thoroughly suspicious now. He turned back to the boy. "Mr. Thouless here accused Gi...Mr. Frost of having stolen something dear to his heart. A silver topped cane with his initial engraved into it."

The boy looked rebellious. "He never stole nothing in his life," he repeated. His little face was black, not just with grime, but with fury. "This cane. Some shiny black wood, is it? And the letter is kind of fancy? Like bird's wings?"

Redfern nodded. *How the devil?*

"Well it ain't HIS," the boy said emphatically, "that's for sure. It's Mr. Frost's."

"And that's the problem, I'm afraid," Redfern said kindly. "Mr. Frost said the same thing. It's his word against Mr. Thouless here, and I'm afraid..."

"Oh you don't have to spell it out for me, sir. I gets it. He's rich and the guv didn't have two pennies to weigh down his purse most of the time. So HIS word is believed and Mr. Frost's good name..." Thouless gave a bay of derision but he went on, "...is wiped out as if it never was." He glared at Thouless but didn't move from the chair. "But I can prove it."

"Oh really?" drawled Thouless. "How can you do that, when Frost himself couldn't?"

"I don't know. Leastways, I don't know at all why the guv didn't set things straight. But he could have proved it easy as anything. Same as I can—and will, sir," he looked pleadingly up at Redfern, "If you'll just get the plate the guv did of your house. He gave it to you, didn't he?"

"I can't be bothered with this charade, Joshua. I'll see myself out."

"You'll stay where you are, by God," Redfern

snarled, and pulled the bellrope so violently it was in danger of coming loose from the wall. Peters was duly dispatched to fetch the engraving whilst Thouless and the boy glared sullenly at each other. Redfern could do nothing but watch their animosity and as each moment passed, he felt more and more like he'd done something spectacularly stupid, and that he'd never be able to put it right.

Peters propped the plate up on a chair.

"You have to know where to look," the boy said, "'cause it ain't never in the same place. But that cane was just about the only thing that the guv had from his dad, you see. Other than the press, of course. And he treasured it. I heard of some artists who always put a dog or a mouse in their pictures. I thought it daft."

He drew a grubby finger down a line of the engraving and Redfern's eyes opened in surprise. What had, until the boy had pointed it out, previously looked like the edge of the wall with a rose trailing over it was now inescapably a walking stick with a silver top, engraved with a fancy initial *F*.

"But with the guv, it's that cane. It's in every piece he ever did. You see? Clever he is, the guv. He liked doing the silhouettes," he said, accusingly, "because he didn't have to work at hiding the cane. Just put it into the subject's hands. That's why he took that man there up on his commission, I reckon. Also, being a friend of yours, like—I think he thought you'd be pleased."

There was a terrible silence and Redfern didn't

know what to do first. Hug the boy, shoot Thouless or shoot himself.

"What's your name, boy?" he said, hoarsely.

"Mordecai, sir."

"Mordecai. Would you go and find my butler
and ask him to come back in?"

When the door closed, Redfern turned slowly
around. His voice was scarcely under his own
control. "Did you break his press, Finn? And for
God's sake, don't lie to me again or I swear I will
kill you where you stand."

"Of course I didn't, you fool."

"Finn..."

"Oh, I *had* it done, of course. The arrogant little slut had been selling himself all over town and
you were too love-struck to see it. I offered him a
commission and he came running like a bitch in
heat. I thought I was doing you a favour."

Redfern gave a laugh, half relief, half horror.
"And he turned you down, didn't he? You tried to
take what he didn't want to offer and he turned
you down flat. That's why you punished him. Oh
God! How could I have been so blind? And he
never told me—not because he was ashamed of
himself, because he was ashamed of you being my
friend! At least he had better taste—better judge-
ment than I, because he wasn't fooled by you—
and I have been all this time. Me and half of London. Well, not one moment more."

"Joshua—"

"Oh don't panic, man. London isn't going to
care one whit about a stolen cane—and I'm not
likely to be letting the *ton* know that a beautiful

young man preferred my advances over yours. London can take itself to hell, for all I care. They'll find you out sooner or later. Now get out."

As if listening outside the door, the butler and Mordecai re-entered. "Mr. Thouless is just leaving, Peters. Please see him out, and Mordecai...make sure he *only* takes his coat, gloves and hat, will you?"

CHAPTER TWELVE

edfern sank back into his chair and buried his head in his hands. He'd been a first-class idiot. He'd had Gideon here, in his house, and now he knew the printer had come to him almost as a last resort. He'd had no choice. He'd lost everything and instead of offering an investigation, friendship and aid, all he'd done was give him paid employment. Treated him like a servant. Then worse, as good as forced him into sex and treated him like a whore. It was obvious to Redfern now—how could he have been so blind? How could he not have recognised the look on Gideon's face, the last time he saw him? It wasn't guilt. It was disappointment. Disappointment in *him*.

The door opened and the boy came in again. He looked a little cleaner and a lot happier. "He ain't half got some fancy swear words, that devil," he said cheerfully. "But I reckon you won't be seeing him again."

The boy was his only hope, and he was almost frightened of asking the question in case he got the answer that he was dreading. "Mordecai, where is Mr. Frost now? Do you know?"

"Not exactly, sir. But my new guv'nor, that's Mr. Verney—the sweep, sir—he must've seen him. He told me what had happened. He said that Mr. Frost had often talked of joining up, you know when money got tight and we was eatin' cabbage and not much else."

"The army?" Redfern's world dropped away in terror. "Surely not? Not him?"

"Yes, sir. He'd said as much to me, but only once. His granddad was a soldier, he said."

"But he could already be..."

"But he might not be, too, sir. Gotta have a bit of hope, eh? But I think we might hurry?"

Minutes later Mordecai had found a cab and they were advancing, as fast as Redfern's bribes would allow, upon Hyde Park and the barracks. Mordecai seemed a little seasick by the vastly bumping coach and was uncharacteristically (from Redfern's short acquaintance) silent. It seemed to take an age before they cleared Gloucester Road and pulled up at the barracks gate, but Redfern leapt from the plate, instructing the boy to keep the cab there. "However long I am away," he ordered. As he strode away, he could hear the cabbie muttering, "Lor, I hope he don't mean to be all night..."

An hour later, and Redfern was wondering how anyone lived long enough to ship overseas and fight, for his short exposure to the military en masse had convinced him that they all needed shooting. They had been singularly unhelpful. As Redfern could not claim to be a relative of Mr. Frost, they said they were unable to give out any information as to whether he had enlisted or not. Perhaps the gentleman could clarify the relationship between himself and Mr. Frost? *You see sir,* (and he had had it explained several times by several ranks) *a lot of men run away from their creditors you see—and if we was to give out that information to all and sundry, well, you'd see where we'd be, sir. Don't you? Leave your card, sir, and if Mr. Frost was to come along and do his patriotic duty* (the implication that Redfern should be in uniform was very clear) *then we'd let you know, perhaps. Yes, there are several Mr. Frosts already enlisted this month, sir, and no, we can't give you more details. Plus, of course sir, it's not unusual for a man to give a false name, had you considered that?*

No, Redfern had not, and after several hours of warming wooden benches with his arse, and speaking to less and less helpful uniformed ninnies, suffering hours of disinterested unhelpfulness, he had no recourse but to give in. Not for the first time in his life, he longed to have the ease of speech and affable charm of Thouless, for the oily bastard would have run rings around the officious brick wall that protected the barracks, and would have the information already.

Defeated, he made his way back to the cab. It was snowing hard at last, and the air felt warmer than it had for weeks. Advising the driver there was now no hurry, they made the trek back to Redfern's house. It wasn't until they were there that Redfern thought of Mordecai and where he'd want to be taken.

"It's all right, sir," the boy said, sadly. "My gang ain't too far from Soho Square today, I can walk from here. I'm sorry, sir. I was sure he'd be there."

"He could well be," Redfern said, heavily. "But they were right not to tell me. Blast them. Thank you, Mordecai. You've saved me from myself today, and if you ever need anything, you come to me."

"I will, sir. But I'll be all right, sir. An' if I hear anything?"

"Yes. Thank you." It seemed odd that it didn't feel strange to be talking to the boy almost like an equal and for one moment, Redfern was unwilling to let the boy go. He was his only link to Gideon, the only one he could have talked to about him. But he opened the door and let the boy out, then watched him as he disappeared into the swirling snow.

A week later he had exhausted all other means of finding Gideon. He had the feeling that the man had actually signed up under a false name, or he had slid between the cracks of London like so many did when all their options had faded away. Redfern had been back to the little shop each day, but it remained locked and shuttered; there were no signs of life except for the presence of a mangy cat who sat on the doorstep as if guarding the door.

On the eighth day, Redfern didn't see the point of going back again. If Gideon had got any of the letters he'd left, he wasn't responding and Redfern knew he'd just have to learn to live with the fact that he'd made the biggest mistake of his life.

As the river-ice melted and London returned to normal, Redfern tried to return to the threads of his life, but every time it snowed he found himself staring out into the garden, remembering the Frost Fair and a man who he'd never forget.

One day at the end of February, he was in his study watching the snow, lost in his thoughts. The flakes were huge, piling up in drifts and topping the laurels like the brightest icing.

The thought of Gideon, homeless in weather like this, cut him to ribbons. All he could hope was that he was somewhere warm, somewhere...somewhere where he was being treated like a decent human being.

Suddenly he caught a movement; a figure in the snow outside, the gardener no doubt, brushing the snow from the paths, but as Redfern glanced again he noticed that the man had no broom, and was taller and leaner in build than the gardener ever was. With his heart in his mouth, he wiped the ice and condensation away from the window, but when he peered once more through the pane, the figure was gone.

With his heart beating wildly and hardly daring to hope, he dashed through the house to the garden door, pulled it open, and raced out into the

white landscape, uncaring that the snow was an-
kle deep and was ruining his shoes and stockings.
He reached the window he'd been standing at and
followed the line of sight from where he'd been sitting. Tracks. Footprints. Bootprints in the snow.
Eyes on the ground, he followed them around the
house and then suddenly there the man was. Just
a dark figure sheltering under the great yew by
the fence between the house and the church.

There was no doubt it was Gideon. He looked
tired and pale but no less himself than when Redfern had seen him last. Wherever he had been, he
had not suffered physically. And he was smiling.
Redfern approached him almost timidly, as if
Gideon was some sprite or snow-mirage that
might vanish if touched. Flakes had settled on
Gideon's hair where it peered beneath his hat,
adding to the fantastic effect.

"I thought—Mordecai said you—I thought
you'd gone."

"I hear that you threw the bastard out,"
Gideon said. "I'm glad for that."

"Gideon. I should have seen the truth of him. It
took a mere boy to make me see it. I'm ashamed
of that. I'm ashamed of everything. Come in,
Gideon, please. It's bitter out here."

"I should not have lied to you."

"Rubbish! Stop it. I was the one who wronged
you. I should have trusted you. I love..."

"Don't say anything."

"Come in, please."

Gideon reached across and as natural as
breathing, took Redfern's hand. Redfern thought

his heart would stop. "I want to, Joshua. But I won't come in as an employee...or a whore. I have a job as a partner in a firm. Not something you'd like; it's not gentleman's work, like printing. But it's honest, and I'm independent. I want to stay that way. Can you be friends with someone like that? Can you manage to take me on those terms?"

Joshua would have taken him on any terms whatsoever, but he could tell how fragile this moment was, how Gideon was likely to melt away into the snow if he thought for one moment that the respect he demanded wasn't there. Joshua wanted to throw the world at Gideon's feet, but knew now that would only scare him off. He took a breath, a breath which burned his lungs with freezing air, and struggled to say in a sentence what he knew that his heart had been saying since he'd lost his love. "I won't take anything that you don't give me freely, I'll never doubt you again."

The sun came out in Gideon's smile, and the snow seemed to melt from the world as Gideon stepped into his arms.

⁂

At first it was tentative, shy, and awkward. After Joshua led him upstairs and locked the bedroom door, he had turned to Gideon and hesitated, as if the small patch of carpet and floor between them was as dangerous as the gulf that had kept them apart. It took Gideon to cross it, Gideon to raise a finger to Joshua's mouth to stop him speaking. They'd done enough of that, and they'd do more, much more later. Then Gideon took the lead; kissing, undressing, whispering small, soft words of lust and need: words of reassurance and encouragement. Together they moved to the bed, naked and clinging to each other, as each kiss became longer and more forceful than the one before. Gideon let the rising tide of Joshua's passion sweep over him as his lover's hands and lips claimed his flesh, nipping, tweaking, *licking* until Gideon thought he'd lose himself and would be happy to be so lost. Lower and lower he went, and Gideon was crying out with need by the time Joshua brought his mouth down to the hollows of Gideon's hips, but still he held off from sliding Gideon's cock between his lips.

When Gideon pleaded, begged, he heard Joshua chuckle, but then to his frustration he felt his lover pull away, just for moment, but he was back almost immediately and with gentle but firm hands he placed Gideon's legs against his body.

"Yes," was all Gideon said, and that's all he could say, repeating the word over and over and over as Joshua's fingers opened him, set a rhythm, then worked him until he had to push his hand against his mouth to stop from crying out. "Yes. And yes. And please." He closed his eyes then, for the sensation and the movement and fire, deep inside, were the call of a drum that could not be ignored, then the warm, blunt feel of Joshua's cock was against his skin, then inside, joining them into one, saying more than words would ever say.

He heard Joshua calling his name, as if from a

distance, felt Joshua's hand take hold of his cock and he tried to answer but it was too late. All he could do was let his orgasm take him, pushing him over the highest of cliffs. It seemed as if he was falling, gently and perfectly into Joshua's arms. The last thing he remembered before he slept was Joshua's mouth against his cheek, and being told how much he was loved.

And much, much later, as the sun pushed the snow from the eaves and the light crept across the wooden floor to where they lay on the bed, entwined, entangled—Gideon let his breath synchronise with Joshua's, then rolled over and put his head on Joshua's chest. He closed his eyes in torpid happiness as he felt Joshua's arms close tighter around him, as if he would never let him go again, and with a silent thought to St. Jude, Gideon prayed that Joshua never would.

The End

An excerpt from

Blessed Isle

by Alex Beecroft

a novella included in

Hidden Conflict
Tales from Lost Voices in Battle

Coming soon from
Cheyenne Publishing
and
Bristlecone Pine Press

Chapter One

I look on the man sprawled face down among tangled bedclothes. The night air is sticky, airless, almost as hot as the day. I'm sat here at the desk, sleepless from the heat, as I will be until dawn brings a breeze from the sea, the scent of tar and ships, and a faint cool. I'll sleep then. For now, I'll light a candle, take out this journal and write. And look at him.

Gauze curtains hang around the bed, milky, ghostly, veiling him. He's kicked off everything but the tail end of a sheet and has hidden his face in the crook of his arm. His back is pale as milk and, in the candlelight, a sheen of sweat gilds his muscles with dim gold. He is a tall man, lithe and slender, and his black hair gleams like jet, curling into the nape of his neck, where a final lock kicks up like a drake's tail.

I lean down to rest a hand gently on his bare shoulder, and he shifts without waking towards the touch. I wonder then, how did I come here? What strange movement of the heavens or gamble of Providence marked me out to be so blessed?

I edge the sash a quarter inch further open, letting in lush, choking air and a multitude of Saint Sebastian's insect life. The pages of my journal lie limp and damp, and the ink sinks thirstily into them. Only a week ago, I examined

a ship trading ice out of Greenland, crawled about
the hold and parted the woven mats of straw to
touch its weeping sides and feel its burning chill
with my fingertips. It was the first and last time I
have been cold in almost a decade.

There might be some relief from this pressing
humidity in the tiny boathouse beneath our tiny
house. The thought of taking candle and journal
and sneaking down there to write in the cool, is
attractive. But it would mean leaving him alone,
and I begrudge every moment spent out of his
presence. We have been forced to give up so much
for this, our state of near-married bliss. Best appreciate it now, lest tomorrow the hangman
snatch it away.

Oak apple gall and vinegar scent drifts sharp
from the ink. I sand the page again and smooth it
as I wonder why I want to leave this record. Why
not leave our story untold? It is dangerous to
speak, let alone to commit the words to paper. My
need to confess may be the death of us both. But it
leaves a bad taste in my mouth that this love
should go unrecorded; that posterity should judge
men like myself—like him—by the poor fools
driven out to grope strangers in alleys, all fum-
bling fingers and anonymous grunting. Those of
us uncaught must perforce be silent. But one day,
perhaps, when the world has grown kinder, this
journal will be read by less jaundiced eyes. To
them I will be able to say there was fidelity here,
and love, and long-suffering sacrifice, and joy. To
them I will be able to speak the truth.

I trim my pen and dip it. From the waterfront,

the docks and warehouses all about us, comes the clap of rope against mast, and laughter; the riot of sailors trying to forget. In the town beyond, the notes of a cavaquinho fall like silver raindrops into the night. But, floating over all, from the hills of the interior comes a rumbling throb of drums as the slaves and the natives too remember their stories, keep their truths alive.

I should introduce myself. I am Captain Harry Thompson of His Majesty's Royal Navy. I began my life as a Norfolk wherryman's son. Pressed aboard the *Sovereign* under Captain Garvey at the age of fourteen, I took to the Navy as a bird, falling from its nest, takes to flight. It was my element and my delight. I filled my hours with work and study. Alone in my hammock at night, I imagined myself a great admiral, pacing the deck of a First Rate, his own flotilla following in strictly measured line behind him. By diligent study of those better born than myself, I polished my manners and my mode of speech, so that I could pass as a gentleman, and thus, in the year 1784 I was made lieutenant. The most junior lieutenant of the *Barfleur* under Sir Samuel Hood.

A man, like myself, with no family connexions, may serve his whole life as a lieutenant, but I was determined that should not be my fate. If I required either a miracle or an act of heroism to secure me a captain's rank, I would produce one. Looking back, I see my hubris plain, but at the time it seemed inevitable that my mere intent should oblige the world to satisfy it. So when, some years later, a French cannonball shattered the railing of the *Barfleur*, bursting into thrumming, foot-long splinters of sharpened oak that sprayed the quarterdeck like spears, I was ready. I stepped in front of the Admiral and received through my shoulder the dart that would otherwise have pierced his throat.

I remember the blur of the sky, hazy, hot and deep, deep blue, all the masts bowing in towards me as if falling atop my face. I felt a crushing sensation as though they had indeed pinned me beneath them, and my mouth filled with blood. I am pleased to say, I could not have cried out even if I had tried. I fell silently into oblivion. And then I awoke in my hammock with a vast pain, and an Admiral in my debt.

Which may be taken as sufficient explanation for why, at thirty-four years of age, with a new wig atop my freshly shaved head, and a servant going on before me to carry my baggage, I took possession of my first, and last, command.

HMS *Banshee*, a sloop of war, swung about her anchor rope in Plymouth that day under gentle English May-day sunshine, and looked as though she had sailed straight out of my boyish dreams. Her paint shone bright azure and gold, and her company, drawn up for my inspection, stood neat and biddable, the officers glittering, the men like a country garden in bright check shirts and ribbons.

I found, later the same day, that she was elderly, had been much knocked about in the Bay of Biscay, and was a leaky, wet ship. Always three feet of water in the well, no matter how we pumped. Always mildew on the food and in our clothes, and her finely dressed men wheezed and coughed as they worked.

My servant unpacked my things and did his best to make the cabin homelike, wiping the black bloom of mould from all the surfaces, installing my few belongings in this sumptuous, almost indecent expanse of private space.

That week I was too full of work to see either officers or men as more than brief, bipedal shadows cast into the cave of my preoccupation. I had a convoy to organise. News had reached London that Captain Arthur Philip had successfully brought his fleet to Rio de Janeiro and, after reprovisioning there, had departed for Australia, his small payload of convicts largely intact. The birth of a new colony was underway, and I was directed to follow with a second fleet, comprising the convict transport vessels *Drake*, *Quicksilver* and *Cornwall*, the supply ship *Ardent*, and the *Banshee* as escort and protector. All this I was to organise myself, and to achieve before the month was out.

In my zeal, I drove myself to achieve it all within the week. I wonder now, looking back, whether—had I taken longer, been more scrupulous—I might even then have seen the seeds of the great calamity to come. A bruise here, a livid cheek there, among the men and women huddled behind iron bars in the holds of the transport ships. Doctors assure me the malady could not have lain low so long, but I cannot help but wonder...

Yet hindsight makes Cassandras of us all, encouraging us to cry out "You should have listened", when it is far too late. Perhaps the doctors are right, and my fault came later. It is my fault, just the same.

The weighed anchor rose with a pop and a spout of bubbles from the decaying detritus that lay on Plymouth seabed. The day was fair, crisp and golden as white wine and the breeze fresh. A Thursday, it was washing day aboard the *Banshee*, and we departed to our fate with the ensign flying, our fleet following, white sails bravely spread, and our rigging fluttering with shirts, small clothes and stockings hung out to dry.

Now, I thought, taking a turn at the wheel to see how she handled—she wallowed like a swimming cow—*I have the time to get to know my ship, my men.*

The spray flew up like silver lace about the yellow haired, screaming woman of *Banshee*'s figurehead. The wind strengthened and the ropes of her rigging creaked with accustomed strain. By afternoon we were out of sight of land. Our little community of ships sailed alone on the deep blue waves of the Atlantic, under a sunset as juicy orange-pink as a peach.

A great burden fell away from me then, and I sighed as the wind nudged my back and whipped the ends of my ribbon against my cheek, the land and its scurry behind me, a long, long voyage before. A journey to the ends of the earth and back. *Now there is time to do more than merely work. Time to live.*

The washing came down from the rigging. The watches changed, last dog watch into First watch. The ship's bell sounded out once, soft and silver over the sigh of waves, and in echo came the sweet ring of the bells on *Drake* and *Ardent*, and a moment later the distant ting of *Quicksilver* and *Cornwall* further behind. Night fell with the lazy downward drift and the sheen of a falling magpie feather.

After eating my solitary dinner, I set my wig on its stand, took off my uniform coat and substituted an old grey short-jacket, disreputable and comfortable. I intended my officers to know at a glance that this was an informal visit. The officer on watch, Lieutenant Bailey, I believe, attempted to hide his lit pipe behind his back as he snatched off his hat with the other hand. I gave him a nod and walked past, pretending not to have noticed, while he pretended not to give my departing back a half salute of gratitude.

I have been down many a companionway—one hand for the ship and one for myself, leaning back to place my weight more firmly on the treads. I don't believe I was aware this was the last time I would do so in possession of my own soul. Not even when I paused outside the closed door of the wardroom at the sound of a voice singing, a voice as smooth and rich as a flagon of whipped chocolate, did I imagine that my life as I had known it was about to come to an end.

A wardroom servant, coming out burdened with dishes, held open the door for me, supposing me too grand to work the latch myself. I ducked beneath the lintel and froze there as if the air had turned to amber. I breathed in scented resin and eternity.

Scattered pewter plates reflected the light from the series of lanterns swinging gently from the beams overhead. The hull curved in about the room like cradling palms. Down the long sweep of table, glasses glittered with pinpricks of silver, the wine within them burning red. *He* stood behind his empty seat at the head of the table, singing.

Braced, his long fingers curled over the back of the chair, the fall of his frock coat devastatingly elegant, he stood like the Archangel Gabriel before Mary. And his beauty was such that had he looked at me and said, like an angel, "Do not be afraid" I would have been obliged to him for the needful reassurance.

Words cannot do him justice. What word is 'black' to describe hair as glossy as obsidian, as soft and thick as fur? He wore it uncovered, unpowdered, in the new, French fashion. It lay straight over his brow, though damp had begun to curl and feather the very ends. His top lip was the shape of a Mongolian recurve bow, only a shade or two pinker than his strikingly pale skin. A stubborn jaw outlined in shadow and a long straight nose. Black lashes and strong black brows. A masculine face, and yet exquisite; clear and glorious as a sword thrust through the heart. I gasped at the shock and ecstasy of it, and without faltering in his song—to this day I don't remember what it was he was singing; "You gentlemen of England" perhaps—he turned to look at me.

His eyes were dark brown, like his voice—like chocolate. Their gaze at first conveyed frankness, thoughtfulness, though with an element of wariness admixed. I saw them widen as he comprehended the interest in my gaze. His song faltered. He licked his lips to moisten them, and a wave of heat and blood rose stinging and tingling to rush gloriously from the soles of my feet to my head. My heart beat twice in silence, the world falling away from our tangled glances, the two of us alone in the pupil of God's eye.

And then normality returned with a chorus of clinks as the slouching officers set down their spoons and cups, leapt to attention, mobbed me with welcomes and glasses of wine.

I couldn't remember his name! We must have been introduced a week ago. One of those dutiful faces beneath cocked hats must have been his. But, distracted by duty, I had been deaf and blind. Impossible though it seemed now, I simply had not noticed.

"Lieutenant Garnet Littleton, sir," he said, and gave me a wry, sensitive smile that made me choke on my claret. Dear God, so much for time! The voyage had only just begun and already I was doomed.

Chapter Two

You cannot guess how I am laughing now in my heart. Well, why should you? I am dead and dust, and all you see is the change of writing from Harry's crabbed scrawl to my elegant hand. There will be fewer ink splots in this portion, I promise you.

Every night it is the same! We tryst with great mutual pleasure, and I, sated, fall asleep, only to be awoken in the grey of dawn by a flutter of curtains, a cold wind and the sound of his snoring. Yet again, he's slumped over the desk, tallow from the candle overflowing the tin saucer in which it stands and greasing his head and elbow. His fingers are in the ink. I have become quite the expert at hauling him from chair to bed and tucking him in without waking him.

Then I sit, and read what he has been saying, and chuckle to myself. He's so earnest! So pedantic. So convoluted in his meaning and expression! I love him for it, but still I laugh.

Look here where he has said. "I don't remember what it was he was singing." Is that not shocking? It reminds me of my father, trying to recount his own courtship over the dinner table. "Your mother was the most radiant creature I have ever seen," he would say, "in a blue satin dress that matched her eyes…"

"Darling, it was teal," my mother would reply. "And silk. I can't believe you can't even remember my dress. Thank God one of us was paying attention!"

And they would bicker for the rest of the afternoon, both of them with the same smug smile, taking great pleasure from their children's annoyance.

I feel a little like that now. For the song was *Give me but a Friend and a Glass, Boys*, and it was flung out like a net to see what I could catch. In case it is not sung where you are, dear reader, here are the words.

Give me but a friend and a glass, boys,
I'll show you what t'is to be gay;
I'll not care a fig for a lass, boys,
Nor love my brisk youth away.
Give me but an honest fellow
That's pleasantest when he is mellow
We'll live twenty-four hours a day.

You see? I was angling for a fish to bite, so I shall not rebuke him too much for being unaware of the lure, when he took it down whole and was hooked. Evidently he was so dazzled by my numerous and wondrous qualities, that my message utterly passed him by. I find I can forgive him for that.

Do you think I'm a fool? Yet it isn't folly which makes my words so light, and causes nonsense to spill out of my mouth like the notes of an aria. It's just that I'm happy. I didn't believe it possible to be this fortunate in life, being what I am. But I was wrong. Happiness goes to my head like wine. I daresay I am insufferable with it. If that's the case, I ask you to bear with me. I will become much more miserable presently.

I suppose I should cease this drivel and pick up the account where Harry has left it off. That momentous instant when Cupid's arrow pierced us both. Straight through one heart into the other, it flew. Metaphorically speaking, you understand, though, at the time, had I looked down and seen blood, I would not have been surprised. The rosy dimpled boy, having done his worst, clapped his bow back between his wings and flew off, chuckling. I was left trying not to smile, trying not to flirt or to stare. Trying not, in short, to get the pair of us hanged.

CPSIA information can be obtained at www.ICGtesting.com

232950LV00004B/26/P

9 780979 777325